AMISH MAYHEM (AMISH ROMANCE)

BOOK 12 THE AMISH BONNET SISTERS

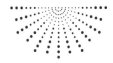

SAMANTHA PRICE

D1715326

CHAPTER ONE

$\mathcal{C}$herish couldn't believe it. She looked down at the paper in her hands.

It was her father's will.

She had never known of its existence. If she or her sisters had known about it, things in their lives would've been very different.

This meant Wilma, their mother, was a dreadful person. She had known about the will. She had to have, since it had been stored in her special box.

With the will firmly under her arm, Cherish flung open the front door of the house and with Caramel, her beloved dog, beside her, she headed into the orchard without closing the door behind her.

Things like closing doors and behaving properly didn't matter anymore. Not to Cherish. Not since realizing her mother had done this. There was only one thing she cared about right now and that was setting things right—the way they should've been.

She looked down at Caramel trotting beside her as she stomped away from the house. "I've got to right the wrongs done by *Mamm*, Caramel. The orchard should've been Florence's all the way along. Everybody knew it. Even Florence felt it in her heart that it should've been hers, I know she did. Florence didn't need to leave it at all when she fell in love. Not really, because everything was hers all along. Well, it should've been—she just didn't know it. Now she's about to find out."

Caramel, panting and smiling his dog-smile with his tongue hanging out one side of his mouth, kept up with his owner's fast strides.

Cherish didn't know much about the legal implications of wills, but she was sure that having been named as executor, her mother was under some kind of obligation or duty to carry out the will to the letter. But the further Cherish walked, the sicker she felt. She didn't want to make an error in judgment and cause her mother and the whole family stress.

Cherish slowed her pace, and then settled herself to sit under one of the apple trees. With her full dress and her apron spread over her knees, she unfolded the will to read it again. This time, more carefully. Her mother always said she charged at things like a bull before thinking.

Perhaps she'd read it incorrectly, or missed something.

Caramel sat down beside her placing his head in her lap.

Cherish blinked a couple of times and then started reading from the top.

It was written fairly plainly with little legal jargon. It still said what she thought it had.

The entirety of the orchard was left to Florence with the rest of the family to have a home there in the large house for the rest of their days. She read it through once, and she read it again from beginning to end.

It still said the same thing. Not a word about Wilma, only to name her as executor.

Cherish double-checked the date.

The will was made about a year before *Dat* died.

Looking out across the peaceful orchard with no one about, Cherish rested her head back on the tree trunk. She knew why Florence felt like she did about the place. The orchard was like a living and breathing thing.

It pained Cherish that her mother was such a disappointment. Old people were supposed to be honest and law-abiding, especially parents.

Yet, why did her mother hold everyone to such a high standard when she obviously had no standards of her own?

Cherish folded the will once more as she remembered all the times that *Mamm* had labeled her uncontrollable. She'd been packed off to Aunt Dagmar's farm on the other side of the world as punishment for a series of wrongdoings. Well, it wasn't exactly the other side of the world, but that was what it had felt like when they were sending her there as punishment.

The more Cherish thought about it, the more she felt all the adults in her life weren't up to standard. They'd all let her down. Her father had died way too young, her mother had married Levi—that was a disappointment and a half. And, Florence had left her and her sisters to run away to marry Carter.

Not that she blamed Florence too much. She would've done exactly the same given half a chance. She was sure her father couldn't help dying, but the feelings in Cherish's heart were ones of abandonment. She'd felt like an orphan when he died, and those feelings had echoed once more to haunt her when Florence had left.

Cherish groaned, disturbing her dog who looked up at her.

Cherish patted him on the head. "It's okay. I'm okay. No one's to blame for what they've done, but even so, they've all let me down. That's how it feels. There's no one who's always there for me. Aunt Dagmar was, but now she's gone too. You're the only one who loves me, Caramel."

Caramel put his head back down in her lap and she smoothed her hand over his soft head.

"When I'm officially an adult, I'll do what I want to do. Live how I want. I wonder if I'm doing the right thing giving this will to Florence? The will did say to give us a home, but it said nothing of Levi because *Mamm* hadn't married him back then, of course, because *Dat* was still alive."

She looked across at the dappled light falling through the leaves of the apple trees.

"Now Levi thinks he owns the land by the way he talks. I didn't find anything amongst their papers to say Levi was the owner. There was no deed, no contract, no paperwork. So Levi must talk as if he owns that because he's a man and he thinks he owns everything that his *fraa* owns, but he doesn't. He doesn't own the orchard. But he might as well because he makes all the decisions."

She scratched her back where some bark was sticking into her and irritating her skin.

"Except he allowed me to make that decision regarding when to start the harvest. Maybe Levi's not so bad. He's also giving Joy and Isaac his house to live in. That was nice."

Cherish remembered how horrible it had been when her mother first married Levi. He and *Mamm* didn't get along at all at first, and Levi even complained to the bishop about Wilma.

Perhaps he'd seen Wilma's true colors. Cherish stared at the document in her hands. Had Levi seen Wilma's muddy and murky colors that she was just starting to see?

Looking up at the sky once more, Cherish wondered if her father knew what was going on. Did he know that Wilma had pushed aside his will and left it forgotten in a box on the top shelf of her closet? In her heart, Cherish knew she'd found it for a reason.

"We have to get this will to Florence." She stood up and just as she was about to walk toward the cottage where her half-sister lived, she spotted Morgan, one of their horses. He was out of the barnyard and chewing on one of the apple trees.

This wasn't good.

The horses were kept in large barnyards and pastures, with plenty of room to graze and move about. They had their stalls too, where they could sleep or hide from unpleasant weather. Sometimes all they wanted was to figure out how to get on the other side of their fence so they could munch on the apples.

She pushed the will down the front of her apron and set off to get Morgan back in his barnyard. Firstly, she needed some rope. The horse wasn't going to follow her, or do what he was told, willingly. That, she knew from past experience. What she needed was a rope or a lead. She ran to the barn, and the first thing she spotted was a discarded length of twine, used to hold the bales of hay together. It was a good length, plenty for what she needed. She hurried through to the back of the barn into one of the stalls that led out into the barnyard.

Then she saw the spot where Morgan had gotten out. The top rail had been pushed down and he'd stepped high over the bottom railings.

With Caramel following her, she got to the broken fence, climbed over it and headed to Morgan. "Come here, boy."

He didn't even look around. She was able to pat his shoulder, and then slip the twine around his neck. "Let's go." She moved him away from the tree, and then he walked alongside her as she led him back through the front gate and into his section of the barnyard.

Then Cherish walked to the fence and, using the same twine she'd used on the horse, she tied the fence rail back up. It would do for a day or two until she came back to hammer it in place. She couldn't do it now because she had to get the will to Florence.

Cherish looked around for Caramel in time to see Morgan kick out at him. Now Cherish was confused. Morgan was normally a calm horse and he seemed spooked.

She walked over to check he had enough water in the trough and just as she did so, she tripped on a rock and fell on the ground. Fortunately, she was able to break her fall with her hands.

When she pushed herself up, she noticed part of the ground was wet. Now she had mud on her. "Botheration." That was something her Aunt Dagmar always used to say. She couldn't even brush it off because she'd have dirty hands when she touched the will.

Her heart nearly stopped when she remembered the will.

She gasped and looked down at the front of her apron hoping it wasn't soiled.

It was gone.

Looking around, she saw it wasn't in the barnyard. She ran back to retrace her steps.

It had to be somewhere!

Then she saw it near where Morgan had been eating. It must've slipped out when she was busy trying to get him back.

She reached down to grab it just as a gust of wind swept it out of her reach. "Botheration." Cherish watched her father's will get swept up into the air like a dried-out leaf.

It was odd that it did that.

Was someone angry? Was it her father, or God?

Then it landed on the ground. She ran for it, and made a lunge, but again, it moved on. From there, it tumbled away from her, taunting her by doing summersaults.

She had to get it.

If it got lost or blew away, no one would believe that it ever existed. Her mother certainly would deny its very existence.

Cherish made one more effort and threw herself onto it. Her body landed with a thud onto the hard ground and just as the wind picked up again, she grabbed the will by its corner.

She had it.

Holding the important document in the air so it

wouldn't soil, she scrambled to her feet. Then she ran through the orchard to Carter and Florence's house next door before anything else happened to stop her.

Relief washed over her when she slipped through the barbed wire fence that separated the two properties.

She was nearly there.

Their car was parked close to the house, and that meant they were home. She'd give them the will and she'd no longer be responsible for it.

With the important document held out at arm's-length and with Caramel beside her, Cherish ran the rest of the way to Florence's house. She took a giant leap up the porch steps and landed with a thud on the boards.

To her shock, her foot went straight through the old boards.

She called out in fright as she tried to pull her foot out of the hole she'd just made. Caramel turned and ran.

Just as she was in the most unladylike position with her legs outspread, grabbing at her foot, Florence opened the door.

The will was the last thing on Cherish's mind at that moment.

"Oh no!" Florence yelled out. "Carter," she called over her shoulder. "Come quick and help Cherish."

Just as Cherish pulled her foot back out, Carter appeared.

Now they both stood looking down at her.

"I'm so sorry," Carter said, looking in horror at the damage. He then lifted Cherish to her feet. "Are you okay? Is your leg all right?"

She looked down at her foot and moved it all about. "I'm fine, I think."

"Good. I've been meaning to do something about the boards with wood rot. I didn't know they were that bad."

"No real harm done. Just a couple of scratches." Cherish looked around for the will. It had fallen beside her. She leaned down and picked it up. "I found something very interesting. You've got to see this."

Florence looked at her apron. "What happened to you?"

"I was just wondering the same," Carter said. "You can't have got that dirty from falling through the porch."

Cherish shook the paper in her hand. "This got away from me, and the horse getting out didn't help either. I nearly lost this because it tried to get away from me. Or it could've been *Gott* or *Dat*." From the looks on Florence and Carter's faces, they had no idea what she was talking about.

Florence tried to get a better look at the paper she was swishing about in the air. "What are you talking about, Cherish?"

"*Dat's* will. This is it, his will." She held it out proudly.

"*Dat* didn't leave a will."

"That's where you're wrong. He did and this is it." She continued to hold the will out to Florence feeling relieved she had gotten it there all in one piece and without getting any dirt on it—well, maybe just a little bit on the one corner.

"Let's go inside," said Carter, "and then we'll be able to hear Iris if she wakes."

As soon as they got through the front door, Florence stood there and unfolded the paper. Her eyes traveled up and down and then she looked up at Carter.

"What does it say?" he asked.

"This really is my father's will. I never knew about it. No one said a thing." As she handed it over to Carter, she continued, "It says I'm to be left the orchard. Me and me alone."

Everyone was quiet while Carter read it through. He looked up. "How did you come across this, Cherish?"

"It was in amongst *Mamm's* paperwork in her room."

Florence frowned at her. "What were you doing going through Wilma's things?"

"It was just getting to me that everyone was talking about the orchard as if Levi owned it and I wondered if he did. I thought that if he did, there'd be some paperwork proving it. That's all I was looking for and I didn't find one thing mentioning it. Then I realized he talks as though he owns it because his wife owns it, so naturally he thinks he's in charge."

Florence's face drained of color and she moved to sit down on the couch. With her hand on her head, she said, "I can't believe this. If this is real, it was supposed to be mine."

"Maybe it's not too late," Cherish chirped.

Florence looked up at Carter. "What should we do? Can we take this to a lawyer since Wilma has ignored it? Because that's what it seems like she's done."

Carter sat down next to Florence and put his arm around her. "It doesn't matter. Let's leave things be. So much time has passed since your father has died and so many things have happened."

"It does matter," Florence snapped. "I want my orchard. That's all I've ever wanted."

CHAPTER TWO

*C*herish was shocked to hear Florence speak like that. She was normally so calm and mild-mannered.

If Carter was shocked too, his calm voice didn't show it. "It's just a piece of land. I can buy up more land and we can plant more trees. I can give you everything you want, Florence."

"Not my father's orchard. You can't do that."

In that moment, Cherish's heart broke a little for Carter. She could see the hurt on his face. He was doing his best to provide for Florence, and he had tons of money to do that. Yet, he couldn't give her the one thing she wanted.

It was a little surprising that Florence didn't care about her husband's feelings. Her face was stony and cold as her eyes glazed over. Was that anger she saw on

Florence's face? "Are you two going to get a divorce?" Cherish asked.

They both stared at her looking none too happy.

"No, Cherish," Carter snapped.

Cherish was shocked. He'd never spoken like that either. He'd always been so nice. "Well, *Englishers* do. You've never had an argument that I've heard. Not like *Mamm* and Levi. They've had a lot but they can't divorce. *Englishers* can. Why wouldn't you if you could? There's no law against it,no one telling you that you can't. Divorce is easy, isn't it? Just a piece of paper and then you're free again."

Florence glared at her. "You've got a lot to learn about relationships. We're just discussing something, Cherish. We can disagree on something without it being a complete disaster."

Carter said, "There's nothing wrong with that. We're two different people who come from two different worlds. Florence and I disagree about a lot of things and that's okay."

Cherish raised her eyebrows as she let that information sink in. It sounded more like an argument to her, but she held her tongue. "I should go. I'll leave that will with you," she told Carter, nodding to the will in his hands.

Carter held the will out to her. "You'll have to take it back with you, Cherish. We can't enact the will."

She kept her hands by her sides. "Why? If I take it

back, no one will do anything and Florence will never get the orchard. What do you think, Florence?"

"It doesn't matter what any of us think," Carter told her. "It should be in Wilma's hands. It must be."

"Yeah well it has been and look what happened—nothing, a big zero, round like a duck's egg. I guess duck eggs are not exactly round, more oval, but you know what I mean."

"You'll have to take it back. It's a legal document."

Cherish reluctantly lifted her hand to take the will from him.

Florence moved closer to Carter and put her hand on his arm. "Carter, isn't there something we could do? I have an opportunity to get my father's orchard and that's something I feel strongly about."

He pressed his lips together and stared at the document. "Would you mind if I make a copy of it?"

"Good idea," Cherish said. "I'm pleased everyone will know what *Dat* wanted. How things should've been." Cherish handed it over and then Carter went upstairs with it.

Florence said, "Do you think it's possible that Wilma didn't know the will was there, or that it exists?"

"She knew. How could she not? It was in her box of things. *Dat* would've discussed it with her. You know how he was with details and making sure everyone knew everything about everything."

Florence nodded. "But he never mentioned a will at all. At least not to me."

"He probably wanted it to be a surprise. Did he tell you about any arrangements that might be made after he died, any at all?"

"No. We never talked about it."

"And you always told me he thought you'd be taking over the orchard."

"That's right. He talked as though I would be."

Iris made noises from upstairs.

"She's waking."

"Can I see her?"

"Of course." They walked upstairs to the nursery. A small section of it doubled as a storage room for Carter's office. He had a small copying machine in the corner along with document storage bins.

"There she is. Come to Aunt Cherish." Cherish clapped her hands and reached down and picked her up. "Oh, she looks just like you, Florence. I can't wait until she's talking. Cherish will be her first word."

Florence laughed. "It's a bit of a mouthful for a *boppli*."

"I think it's easy. Cher—ish."

Iris opened her mouth and cried.

"Oh no! She must be hungry."

"She always is when she wakes, but first, I have to change her diaper."

Cherish winced and didn't waste any time handing her over to Florence. Then she headed over to Carter. "I hope you can get the orchard back, Carter, for Florence."

"I guess it's more complicated now. Wilma's married and—"

"What does that have to do with anything?" Cherish asked.

"I'm not sure, but if your father hadn't had a will, everything would've gone to Wilma. Now she's married, if anything happens to her everything that she owns would go to Levi."

"That's not right. And when he dies, Bliss will get it all—our father's orchard. That's so wrong. She doesn't care about the orchard. She only cares about rabbits and the boyfriend she stole from me. No one cares that she stole him. Everyone just pretends it's okay."

Carter frowned at her and Cherish regretted saying that bit about the boyfriend.

Cherish grunted. "It would be a disaster if the orchard fell into Bliss's hands. The rabbits would overflow the orchard and eat everything. They gnaw things with their big teeth until everything's destroyed. That's why *Mamm's* so upset with rabbits in the house and I can't blame her for that. Surely *Gott* wouldn't want that to happen. Besides all that, she knows next to nothing about managing an orchard."

"I'm not a lawyer to know if this will is even valid and I'm not sure what happens after so much time has passed with nothing done." He closed the lid of the copy machine and handed the will back to her. "There, all done."

Cherish waved the will in the air. "So this might be totally useless?"

"We'll go to a lawyer and find out," Florence said.

Carter stared at her. "Are you sure you want to do that, Florence?"

"Just to see where we stand. There's no harm in that, is there?"

"The orchard is home to other people now. Do you really want to upset that? Wilma's married again and so much time has passed, not only for them, but for everyone. We have our own orchard now and the one we bought on the other side of the Baker Apple Orchard."

"The Jenkins' orchard," Cherish said. "The Baker Apple Orchard should've been Florence's orchard though. Think of it, you could combine all three and have a totally massive orchard. You'll still let us all live there, won't you, Florence?"

"Of course. I don't need to live in the house. I just want what's mine, what was my father's. Can't you see that, Carter?"

He frowned at Florence. "We'll talk this over later." Then Carter put his hand on Cherish's shoulder. "I'll show you out. Thanks for bringing this to our attention and sorry you fell through our porch."

Cherish didn't budge. "Levi was thinking of selling,

has been thinking of it ever since he married *Mamm*. What if he sells it? What then?"

"Yes, Carter, he could sell it. Now's our opportunity to act. Thanks for bringing the will here, Cherish."

"You're welcome. I had to when I saw it."

"I'm no lawyer," Carter said, making that point once more, "but I think we'd be doomed if he sells. Unless we want to enter into a messy court case."

Florence sighed. "No, we don't want that. I've only ever wanted a peaceful life, and to have my orchard."

Cherish noticed that Carter's body was rigid. Was he unhappy that Florence was so obsessed with the property that once belonged to her father? Cherish knew how she felt, but she could also see things from Carter's point of view. Were cracks forming in their marriage? Cherish never thought it was possible. "I should go."

"I'll walk you out," Carter said.

"Bye, Cherish, and thanks."

Cherish smiled at Florence, who was in the midst of changing the diaper. "Bye, Florence, bye, Iris. Keep saying Cherish to her. Cher—ish. It should be easy for her to say."

Florence smiled. Normally she would've thought it funny, might've even giggled, but she was too focused on what the outcome of the will would be.

As Cherish walked down the stairs with Carter, she said, "Do you wish I'd never brought the will here?"

"No. It's good for Florence to know her father's wishes. I'm sure that's given her a sense of peace."

"But you don't think it'll ever happen, do you?"

"To be honest, no. Levi has entrenched himself in your lives now and in the life of the orchard. I don't see Wilma wanting that to change. That's probably why she hid the will, if that's what she's done. Also, don't forget that Florence left the community."

"I know but she left the community long after our father died."

"Still, we must consider everyone in this. Florence doesn't need the orchard, and I'm sure Wilma finds stability keeping things as they are. It must provide an income for the family. I know Florence doesn't care about the income and would allow the family to make use of the income, but from what I know of Levi, he wouldn't be happy about it."

Anger rose within Cherish.

She'd just had the opportunity to ruin the harvest and affect the finances of the orchard.

That was what she'd decided to do, so Carter and Florence could buy it when Levi gave it all up. But that sneaky Levi had put her in charge of saying when to start the harvest. He knew everyone wanted him to fail. He'd played on her good nature and her sense of doing what was right. It was as though he knew what was about to happen, what she'd been thinking, even though she'd told no one.

It all clicked into place in her mind as all the pieces

of the puzzle came together. Levi was sneaky. So was Wilma. The pair made a good match.

She reached the front door. "Bye, Carter. What am I supposed to do with this will now?"

"Put it back where you found it."

That was the very last thing Cherish wanted to do. It would go against everything she believed in. "Then everything will stay the same."

"If you tell your mother you know about it, there's a chance she could destroy it and deny its existence."

"Ah, that's why you made a copy?"

He nodded.

"I'll put it back and I'll keep my mouth shut—for now."

He opened the door for her and then moved through it after her. They both looked down at the hole in the porch. "Sorry about that, again."

"It's okay. Barely a scratch on me."

"I'll get it fixed. I'll add it to the never ending list of jobs to do for this old place."

"Um, better put it at the top of that list."

He smiled. "I will."

"Bye."

"Bye, Cherish."

Cherish jumped down from the porch without touching the two stairs. Caramel had been waiting for her on the porch and he quickly followed her. When she was a distance away from the cottage, she said to her dog. "I don't know what they're going to do. Maybe nothing." She thought about her own farm, and who she'd leave it to when she died. The husband she didn't have yet? What if he turned out to be awful after a few years of marriage or even a few weeks? "Another reason not to marry anyone. Can you imagine having a husband who tells me what to do like Levi does with Wilma?"

Dagmar had stayed unmarried, and right now that seemed a sensible choice.

Cherish slipped between the wires of the fence and made her way through the orchard, ignoring the things she saw that needed doing. She also conveniently forgot the top fence rail that needed hammering back into place. It was Sunday, a day of rest, after all.

She walked through the open door of the house, surprised the day's sudden wind gusts hadn't blown it shut. She'd be alone for a good few more hours since everyone was still at the meeting and then they'd stay for the meal afterward. Some of her sisters including Caroline, Favor's pen pal, might stay on for the singing.

Back in her mother's room, Cherish reluctantly placed the will back where she'd found it. It was going to be difficult to keep quiet about it, but she had to do so because she told Carter she would. He was one of the few people who was nice to her so she didn't want to do anything to change that. One day, her mother would be exposed for what she'd done.

Cherish would have to practice patience and see how long it took for the truth to come out.

CHAPTER THREE

*O*nce Florence had found out that she was supposed to get the farm after her father's death, she knew it was an answer to prayer. God had heard her. Even though she'd turned away from the community, He was still with her. She hadn't left Him.

She'd made herself and Carter cups of coffee and then she held Iris in her arms as they sat in the living room to talk things over. Silently, she waited for him to speak first, knowing she had to talk him into doing something about making things right. What exactly, she didn't know, but something had to be done.

"If you've got your heart set on it, I'll do my best to get it for you." He took a sip of his coffee and then reached out and placed it down on the coffee table.

When Iris started making unsettled noises, Florence hoped their conversation wouldn't be cut short.

"All I'm saying is, think it through," Carter said.

"This could do damage to Wilma's family, which is an extension of our family now, too."

Florence kept quiet, fearing if she spoke her mouth would run away with her as it so often did. She'd say something she'd later regret.

Where did Carter's loyalties lie?

What about her feelings?

Carter had to know from the moment he met her that the orchard was everything to her. It had been her whole life.

A small voice told Florence that Carter wanted the best for his birth mother, Wilma, and that was fine, but not when it conflicted with her interests. She had to come first, since she was his wife.

"Say something." He ran a hand over his short hair.

Florence sighed. "You asked me to think it through and that's what I'm doing. Thinking."

"Not right now. I meant over a few days so we don't rush into anything."

"Perhaps we should have Wilma over here and talk it through. Maybe she could come with Levi and we can sit down and talk about it like adults."

Carter shook his head. "I think you're looking at this through rose-colored glasses. If Wilma's hidden the will, she's not going to want to talk about it as though talking about a misplaced fence line. This is the ownership of the orchard. There's also every possibility that she's hidden this from her own husband."

"I see what you mean. I didn't think of that."

"There's so much to think about with this. It might've been best if Cherish had kept it to herself."

Annoyance filled Florence, and she hollered, "No! Don't you want me to have the orchard? It was my father's. It should've been mine, but looks like someone's trying to keep me from having it."

"Lower your voice, Florence, please. I've never heard you like this."

"That's because something like this has never happened."

He frowned, looked at Iris in Florence's arms. "I'll take Iris upstairs. It's not good for her to hear yelling. That's not how I want her raised."

Before Florence could say anything, Carter had taken Iris out of her arms and he was heading up the stairs.

She huffed and walked outside into the fresh air. Spot moved off the couch quick enough to get outside with her before she closed the door behind her.

Everything swam in her head.

Why couldn't Carter understand how it felt to be cheated? Her father wanted her to be the sole owner of the apple orchard. Her brothers weren't interested, and her stepsisters weren't either. And she was sure that Wilma only married Levi because she couldn't handle the workload after she'd left to marry Carter.

Florence recalled many a time since her marriage, she'd walked her land looking at the orchard next door

—the Baker Apple Orchard—praying that it would one day be hers.

Now, this was her opportunity. This was what she'd prayed for. Why was Carter against it? Was he going to block her one, God-given chance to claim it?

God was opening a way. That had to be what was happening. *"Gott* please soften Carter's heart and make him understand how important this is to me. Nothing has to change for Wilma and her family. It seems like Levi's not interested anyway because he's always talking about selling."

Then Florence had a thought. This might open up a conversation she could have with Wilma and Levi, and if she had to pay for the orchard she would. Hopefully, they wouldn't want a ridiculously high price.

Florence reminded herself that Carter had a point, that it was only land and didn't really matter, and she shouldn't get so upset, but when she was younger, she'd tagged along after her father and he had taught her everything. Those were the best days she'd ever had. That was what she wanted for Iris, to grow up walking in the same orchard as she had. It was a legacy; Iris's history.

Wilma had cheated her and her daughter out of it. Bitterness welled up inside Florence. She'd given Wilma and Wilma's six daughters the best years of her life.

She'd slaved in the house as well as working in the orchard and the shop. Then at night, she'd stayed up sewing past midnight when Mercy, the eldest, had grown out of her dresses and needed new ones.

She was the one who had seen to all the girls' needs, and listened to all their problems as well as to Wilma's.

Wilma had done little work, and now to learn her stepmother had taken what *Dat* had declared rightfully Florence's. It was wrong.

Florence was going to right the wrong.

It was going to be unpleasant, but with God, it would all work out in the end.

Soon, Carter stood behind her.

She turned around to face him. "I'm sorry for raising my voice."

"It's something I'm not used to. Don't want to get used to."

"I know."

"She fell asleep as soon as I put her down."

"She must've been tired."

"Florence, if this is what you want, I'll help you get it."

"You will?"

He nodded and then took a step toward her and she collapsed into his arms.

Thank you, God.

Why did she ever doubt him?

CHAPTER FOUR

*O*ver breakfast the next morning at the Baker/Bruner household, Joy and Isaac had joined everyone at the breakfast table. It was moving day for the two of them.

Levi said, "Does anyone know anything about the broken fence in the barnyard? It's been tied with twine."

Cherish had clean forgotten. *"Ach,* sorry, Levi. I totally forgot. When I was home sick yesterday, I looked outside and saw Morgan out. In my weakened state, I managed to get him back. I was too ill to do a proper job of fixing the fence, so I tied the rail back in place."

"Denke, that was good of you."

"I'm sorry. I should've remembered to tell you, or fix it myself. I'm good at things like that. Aunt Dagmar showed me how to repair fences and do a lot of jobs around the place. So, you can punish me if you want for forgetting it."

"*Nee*. It was a good thing, Cherish. It shows you're becoming more responsible. Would you like to help me fix the fence properly later today?"

Cherish was surprised at Levi asking such a thing. She lowered her buttered toast and put it back down on her plate. "I gave my word I'd help Joy and Isaac with their new *haus*. I mean, the one they're moving to. It's not exactly new."

Levi chuckled. "It's quite old. Definitely not new. You're right about that."

"Joy and I will make it like new," Isaac said.

Joy added, "Once the repairs are done, it'll be a fine *haus*."

"I can help you fix the fence before I go," Isaac told Levi.

"*Nee,* it's okay. You've got enough to do."

Wilma said, *"Ach,* you should've had a son, Levi."

Bliss's eyes opened wide, and she said to her stepmother, *"Mamm,* do you think I should've been a boy?"

"Nee, but he could've had another child who could've been a boy."

Isaac said, "Levi, I don't mind helping with the fence. It won't take long."

"Nee and that's the end of it." Levi then stared at Cherish. "Are you well enough to help them move today? You've been so ill."

"I've made a full recovery, almost. I can do as much as I'm able."

Mamm narrowed her eyes at Cherish, and Cherish knew she didn't believe a word. "The girls will have to do your work here for you, Cherish."

"Good."

"Are you quitting your job today, Hope?" Levi asked her.

Hope's shoulders lowered as she slouched further into the chair. "Oh. I was hoping you weren't serious about that."

"I'm deadly serious. I said no more work outside the home. We all need to make this orchard profitable. We can use your help to make goods to sell and then we need you to help sell them."

"I can do that too as well as work. Jane needs me."

Levi's jaw clenched. *"Nee,* she doesn't. She can get someone else. You're only a cleaner. She can get a dozen other girls. It doesn't have to be you. You'll work here with us."

"But, I want to work there. I love everything about it."

Mamm's coffee mug landed heavily on the table in front of her causing everyone to jump. "Clean out your ears, Hope. You heard what Levi said and that's the end of it."

"Can I say one thing?" Cherish said in as meek a tone as she could.

"Nee!" Wilma snapped.

31

"What is it?" Levi asked her as he raised his eyebrows.

Cherish wiped any toast crumbs away from her mouth. "We all know that Hope will soon marry Fairfax."

"We don't know that. He hasn't even been baptized yet. Anything could happen. Nothing is certain in life."

"Hush, Wilma," Levi said, "let the girl speak."

"*Denke,* Levi. What I was about to say was if Hope … I mean, *when* Hope marries Fairfax, she won't be working here will she?"

"She can if she wishes," Levi said. "We'll have enough work. The more everyone produces in the kitchen, the more we have to sell."

"But she doesn't wish. What she wishes is to stay working with Fairfax's aunt in the bed and breakfast. If she wants to do that when they're married, why force her to stop doing it now?"

A hush fell over the table and even Caroline stopped talking as all eyes were on Levi awaiting his response.

Cherish added, "They could only be months away from marriage."

Hope smiled, and *Mamm* scowled.

"I'm the head of this *haus.* I can't be concerned with what one person wants. I'm doing the best for the family as a whole. We are all parts of a whole."

"So, what does that mean for Hope, *Dat?* And can Cherish and I still work at the café because we both love it? We could only work one or two shifts," Bliss said.

"It means no!" Wilma told her.

Bliss shrank down in her chair.

Hope said, "If I have to quit working for Jane, this will be the very worst thing I've ever had to do."

Wilma laughed. "If that's the worst, you've had a very good life."

Hope let out a long sigh. "Can I at least work until she finds my replacement?"

"*Jah*, that would be the decent thing to do," Wilma said. "As long as it doesn't take too long. I'd say a week should be enough. What do you think?" Wilma asked her husband.

Levi nodded. "We all have to pull together, Hope, and you're not married yet and you're still living under my roof."

Cherish glared at him as anger welled inside her.

His roof?

It was really her older half-sister's roof.

Not *Mamm's,* not Levi's, and not anyone else's.

It took all her self-control and then some not to blurt out what she knew. "Excuse me." Cherish got up from the table.

"You're not finished with your food," Bliss told her.

It was rare that Cherish left anything but an empty plate in front of her. "I'm finished. I'm more than finished."

Joy said, "You're still helping me aren't you, Cherish?"

"*Jah*. I'm just going upstairs for a minute. Then I'll be ready to go."

"Good."

As Cherish walked up the stairs, she heard Bliss say, "Aw, I wish I was going."

"You're to stay and help out here," Mamm said.

Cherish flung open her bedroom door and then closed it behind her. Once she was at the window, she looked out. From there, all she could see was the barn, but if she leaned over and looked to the left, the edge of the orchard could be seen. She knew how wretched Florence would be feeling right now about what Wilma had hidden from her.

She pushed open the window to let in some fresh air.

Wilma's deception was something Cherish couldn't get out of her mind, but Wilma wasn't a stranger to secrets. She'd kept many of them and to her ... what was one more?

Yet, this secret involved taking something away from someone.

It was so wicked, Cherish could scarcely believe it. It was something she'd never do and that was why she couldn't imagine her mother doing it.

Giving the orchard to Florence was her father's wish and her mother was going against that. So that meant Wilma was going against her father when she wouldn't go against Levi. The whole thing was awful.

Still, Cherish was pleased she had found the will. That had to make Florence happy, even if she never took it any further.

Cherish couldn't wait to find out what Florence and Carter were going to do about it. She hoped they'd do something.

A knock sounded on her bedroom door. "You ready now, Cherish? Isaac wants to go soon."

"*Jah*, I am."

Joy opened the door. "Are you okay? You disappeared from the kitchen so suddenly."

"Yeah. I just couldn't listen to it any longer. I feel so sorry for Hope. Firstly, Levi wanted us all to get outside jobs and give him the money, which was supposed to be for the family. Now, he's changed his mind and Hope has to leave the job that she wouldn't have gotten if Levi hadn't insisted she do." Cherish drew a quick breath. "That probably didn't make sense. I jumble my words when I'm upset, but do you see what I'm saying?"

Joy sighed. "I know, but he's doing his best. He's not used to having the responsibility of so many *kinner* and such a big orchard. This is all new to him."

"Well, he's doing an awful job."

Joy frowned at her. "Cherish!"

"You always have a way of looking at things to make them seem better."

Joy giggled. "I don't think so. I just try to see things from the other person's side. You could try doing that too. Often in an argument, both people think they're right. You see, they are. Each person believes their side of things, and if you step into their shoes and see things with their eyes, you can be compassionate."

Cherish stared at Joy and wondered what she'd think of their mother when the truth came out.

Joy smiled. "Do you know what I mean?"

"No. Let's get out of here."

CHAPTER FIVE

a couple of Isaac's friends had arrived to help him load Levi's wagon with his and Joy's belongings. The young couple didn't think they owned much, until the wagon was nearly full and the men weren't done yet.

"I don't know where all these things have come from," Joy said as she stood looking on with Cherish.

"You've got a lot of stuff."

"It seems so. How did it fit inside that small caravan? Thanks for coming with me in the buggy. I didn't fancy the idea of going in the bumpy wagon with Isaac and his friends."

"I didn't want that either. It's going to be weird with you living so far away now," Cherish said.

"I'm hardly far. It's only twenty minutes."

"Well that's far to me. Especially when you've been

in the same *haus* all my life ever since I was born, and then you were just over here behind the barn."

Joy covered her tummy with her hand. "With the little one coming, we've out-grown the caravan. We could've made it work, but thanks to Levi, we don't have to."

"Why do you think he's being so nice?" asked Cherish.

Joy laughed. "He's just being generous. He wanted to do something to help us. After all, this is his grand-child too."

"I didn't think of it like that. I guess he won't have a proper grandchild until Bliss gets married. And who knows when that will be."

"I don't think it'll be too far away. She's getting on so well with Adam."

Cherish shook her head.

"Now don't start that again, Cherish."

"Start what?"

"The whole thing where you say that you saw Adam Wengerd first."

"But I did, and he liked me better. I was the one who got the stupid rabbit for Bliss, for her birthday— Cottonwool, Cottonball, or Cottonfluff, whatever she's calling him today."

"Her. It was a female rabbit. Remember all the baby rabbits?"

"I can't very well forget, can I, with *Mamm*

complaining about them every single moment of every single day?"

"I think she's been quite good about it. I wouldn't be happy with animals like that in my house either. Cats and dogs are okay as long as there aren't too many of them, but rabbits gnaw on everything with their big teeth."

"They can't help it," Cherish said.

"I didn't say they could help it, I just said that's what they do."

"You're a bit cranky today. It must be those hormones."

Joy's mouth turned down at the corners. "I'm the same as I've always been. Although it does make me a bit cranky to hear you tell me that I'm cranky, because I'm not."

"I'm sorry then, all right? Does that make you feel better?"

"It does. And if you're going to help me out today, I want you to only speak nice things."

"I always speak nice things."

"No, you don't."

"Well, I try to."

"What about how you're always complaining about your farmworker? What's his name again?"

"Malachi, and I have good reason to complain about him. I'm not complaining for the sake of it. He's making too many decisions on his own."

"Isn't that good, though? You're not there. He can't

be sitting on the phone to you all the day long while you make decisions for him."

"Don't worry about it, Joy. You just don't know what I mean. It's not that situation at all. I can't wait to see this house of yours." Cherish covered her mouth. "Whoops, I mean, Levi's house."

"It'll be our house for the moment. You can call it ours, you don't have to keep calling it Levi's. It needs a lot of work, so don't be too shocked when you see it."

"Nothing about Levi would surprise me and that'll just transfer to his house." Cherish laughed. "I've heard it needs work. As long as you don't mind, I won't mind."

They both looked up when they felt raindrops.

"Ach nee. I hope it doesn't rain too hard. It'll be awful bringing the things into the *haus."*

Then Isaac called out, "You go on ahead, Joy. The door's unlocked and we won't be far behind you."

"Okay." Joy faced Cherish. "Let's go."

"I've been ready for ages."

Isaac had hitched the buggy for them and packed the back of it with their cleaning supplies and kitchen items.

"Come on, Goldie," Joy yelled and then both Goldie and Cherish's dog, Caramel, came bounding toward them.

"Ach, I'll have to close Caramel in the house. He won't understand that he can't come too."

"Okay."

While Goldie jumped up into the buggy, Cherish enticed her dog into the house. Before she left, she called out, *"Mamm,* keep Caramel in here, would you? I don't want him to try to follow us."

Mamm came out of the kitchen wiping her hands. "No need to yell. What are you doing?"

"Caramel won't understand why he can't come in the buggy if Goldie's going with us."

"He's just a dog, Cherish, not capable of thoughts."

Cherish frowned at her mother. "Every animal has thoughts. How else would they survive?"

"They're instincts, not thoughts. Only people think. Just go, Cherish. I'll mind the dog."

There was no point in arguing with her mother. She wasn't going to waste another minute of an exciting day away from home. *"Denke, Mamm.* I won't be long. Wait, I will be gone all day, but you can let Caramel out soon."

"Tell Joy not to forget that she and Isaac are coming back here for the evening meal."

"I'll remind her." Cherish closed the door and ran to the buggy. It was exciting to see Joy and Isaac starting their life together in a brand-new place even if it was an old home, and from what she'd heard, nearly falling down.

She jumped in the buggy with Joy. *"Mamm* says animals don't think."

"What?"

"Don't worry." She dismissed the thought with a little sweep of her hand. "Let's just go."

Joy took hold of the reins and they headed down the driveway.

Cherish had a good look at the shop at the front of the house. A couple was making their way inside. "First customers of the day it looks like."

"I hope the shop does well. It wasn't a good idea to let it sit there closed during these last couple of years. We have to gain back all our old customers."

Cherish noticed Joy looked worried. "It's okay. We will. *Gott* will see to it. Hard work always has its reward."

"You're right." Joy turned onto the road.

As they drove past Florence's cottage, Cherish wondered what was going on. Were Florence and Carter going to do anything about the will?

Anything at all?

She'd heard nothing from them. Keeping what Wilma had done a secret was nearly killing her.

Goldie moved to sit on her lap and Cherish put her arm around him. "I'm looking forward to today. You must be so excited, too."

"I am, but don't be surprised when you see the place."

"You already warned me. How bad can it be?"

Joy sighed. "In the bedrooms the linoleum is all rotted away so bad... There is a hole in the floor in one of the bedrooms."

"I heard about that, but you do get free rent for six months or so, don't you?"

"That's right, in exchange for labor, and maybe a little longer."

Cherish stared at the road ahead. She could never imagine being indebted to Levi. Thanks to Aunt Dagmar, she'd never have to be indebted to anyone. "That's a nice thing for Levi to do."

"It is. I was a little shocked if I'm truthful, which I always am." Joy laughed. "We are going to be doing a lot of work on it, though, so the place will be worth a lot more to Levi when we leave."

"Still, you're getting the better end of the deal. I think so, anyway."

Joy took her eyes off the road to look at Cherish. "Please don't mention that to Isaac."

"Why? Is he too proud? Pride goes before a fall you know." Cherish delighted in quoting scripture back at the sister who was always doing the scripture quoting.

When she saw Joy's mouth curve down at the corners, Cherish felt horrible. "I'm sorry. Of course I won't say a thing, not one thing."

Then tears flowed down Joy's cheeks.

Cherish felt uncomfortable and didn't know what to do. She couldn't hug her because Joy had hold of the reins, and she didn't know what she'd done to make Joy cry. "Is this about what I said?"

Joy shook her head.

"Wait, is the *boppli* okay? Is it hurting you?"

Joy shook her head again.

"Then why are you crying?"

"I don't know."

Goldie licked Cherish's face. "Stop it." She pulled her face away from the dog. "Behave."

"Things are hard sometimes," Joy said with a sniffle.

"What things? Things are good for you." This was not the Joy she knew. Joy normally had an answer for everything. "Is it the rising damp in the house and the leak in the bathroom? At least there is an inside bathroom. No running outside on a cold and snowy night and then the door getting covered in snow before you can get out and then you're locked in the toilet all night."

Joy laughed with a hiccup. "That never happened. You're so silly sometimes."

"It could happen though with an outside toilet … and in the snow."

"The chimney's blocked too," Joy announced, sniffing again and wiping away the last of her tears.

Cherish smiled. "Oh no. That's not good."

"I don't know why I'm like this, Cherish. Sometimes I feel sad and want to cry for no good reason."

"Hormones."

"I don't know. Could be."

"Don't worry about the *haus*. *Mamm* is making the curtains and we'll all help."

"*Denke,* Cherish. You're very thoughtful and kind."

Cherish sighed. "I know. It's true."

"There is a lot of work to do and Isaac can't wait to get started. Levi is paying for all the materials and all Isaac and his friends need to do is the work. We'll make the living room our bedroom until we get the main bedroom ready to occupy. It won't be for long."

"Good." Cherish wondered if Joy was trying to talk herself into liking the place.

CHAPTER SIX

*a*t Florence and Carter's cottage, Florence paced up and down in the living room.

Carter walked in with a cup of coffee and slipped his cell phone into his pocket at the same time. "I just called that lawyer friend of mine and he said it is possible to remove an executor of a will and then an administrator would be appointed. But that would all have to go through court."

Florence shook her head. "I don't want to go to court against Wilma."

"It seems the law firm who drew up your father's will wasn't informed of his death."

"You haven't contacted them, have you?"

"Not yet."

"I would say that would be possible. The Amish don't publish funerals or deaths in a newspaper or anything. It would've been mentioned in one or two of the Amish newspapers, but *Englishers* would never read those."

"That's right." Carter sat on the couch while Florence continued to pace.

"No mention was ever made of a will so I assumed... Well I didn't really assume anything. It never came into my mind. I didn't give anything a thought until Wilma married Levi. No, it was when I left the orchard to marry you. In my head, the orchard was always mine, sharing the proceeds with my family. It was mine in my heart, mind, and soul."

"I know how you've always felt about the orchard, Florence, but that was then and you have a new life now. It would be naïve of you to think everything would stay the same when you left the community. The old saying comes to mind, *you can't have your cake and eat it too*. You made your decision and you left your old life behind."

Florence chewed on a fingernail. "I have done no wrong. It's Wilma who's done wrong."

"Finger-pointing won't help. Things are what they are."

Florence swung around to face him. "Things can be changed, decisions can be reversed. I have another saying for you; *it's not over until it's over*. And, I'm telling you now, it's not over. Not by a long shot."

"I know you don't think Wilma handled things well, but what happened to her can't have been easy. With having me before she was married and having to hide that fact from the community. Then the trauma of giving me up. When someone goes through something like that, it fractures them to the core."

Ripples of annoyance echoed through Florence's body. Many women had been through worse than Wilma. Florence tried to see Carter's point of view as she sat down next to him. "Wilma was always a very nervy woman, prone to lots of illness. She never seemed well."

"There you go. She probably lived under extreme stress." He pressed his lips together, and then continued, "I know Wilma said she told your father she'd had a child before they married, but did you ever consider that might've been a lie?"

The words startled Florence. "No. I never considered it, but it could've been a lie, couldn't it?"

Carter nodded. "It's possible. She lied about me and didn't acknowledge my existence, so she's hardly a stranger to lying. What's another one in the scheme of things? Maybe she was trying to save face and make what happened back then … and make her mistake— me—acceptable to you and to her other daughters by saying your father knew about it and was okay with it."

"It never crossed my mind she'd be lying about that. My father was a very sensible and practical man. I don't think he would've thought any worse of my mother for making a mistake when she was young, but then again, it's hard to tell how someone would react. You've got me thinking. Would Wilma have risked rejection from him if he wasn't happy with the news? Surely, he'd have wondered—where is this child and why isn't Wilma seeing him, or seeing her own sister?"

"With Wilma, anything's possible. I hate to say this, but you can't trust her. I thought that even before I learned about the will. You told me before that she's weak-minded. I don't think she can help herself. Desperate people do desperate things."

Florence knew that Carter was against trying to get the orchard back even though they now knew it was her father's wishes. "Lately, she's been nice to me. She's come to see Iris a couple of times and she even brought my mother's treadle sewing machine back to me. What if it was all just an act?"

"It could be. To cover up how bad she felt about hiding that will for years. That's something we'll probably never know, because she'll never tell us."

Florence tried to steady her breathing.

"I could contact that law firm mentioned on the letterhead of the will. They'll be holding a copy of the will, or perhaps even your father's original one."

Florence held her head. "Not just yet. It is a lot to think about."

"Yes, I know." He put his arm around her. "I want you to have everything, but if you chase after the orchard, you'll be involved with them and they'll drag you down—drag us down. We have enough to keep us busy and soon the foundations will be dug for our new house."

"Maybe you're right. It does make me feel better knowing my father wanted me to have the orchard. I don't know if that's enough, though. Why did I find out about it if I'm not meant to do anything?"

"Because Cherish is a snoop."

Florence laughed and moved away from him. "You know I'm talking about in the larger scheme of things. Did God want me to know that information so I'd do something about it?"

"Maybe He wanted you to know, just so you'd know."

"Gotcha. You said you don't believe in God and here you are talking like He exists."

He laughed. "I was just saying that for your sake. That's what you believe."

Florence shook her head. "I don't think so."

"I've got an open mind. Anyway, keep the information in your head and see how you feel in a few days. A few days either way is not going to matter."

"I hope not."

"It won't."

CHAPTER SEVEN

*C*herish and Joy were nearly at Joy and Isaac's new home.

"It's so exciting, Joy. I really can't wait to see the place. You're blessed to have a husband. A *gut* man who can look after you. You didn't even have to go looking for him. He landed right in your lap." She was trying to make Joy feel better so she wouldn't cry again. She didn't know what to do when Joy cried.

"He did."

Goldie licked Cherish's face again and she pushed his head away. "I wonder how things will be for me." She thought about Daniel Withers, the reporter. That was the man she could see herself with. He was starting out in his career and she could stay home and raise the children while he chased his news stories. She liked and respected men who worked hard. "What if I have to leave the community to find love the way Florence did?"

"*Nee*. I'm sure you won't. Things are different for us. There will be a man out there for you when the time is right, Cherish, not before. You're way too young."

Cherish pressed her lips together. The 'annoying' Joy hadn't taken long to return.

"Isaac might even have a younger friend for you from his old community."

"That's okay. Don't ask him. It'll happen if it's meant. I might end up like Dagmar and be a spinster until the end of my days."

"I've always disliked that word, spinster. It sounds like something awful. Why couldn't someone have found a better word for it rather than spinster? It sounds pitiful or something."

"You could say, single. A single woman. A single or an unmarried woman. Or a miss."

"Anything is better than spinster."

"I agree. It does sound awful." Cherish looked out the window of the buggy feeling glad that she and her sister could agree on something. At least she'd stopped crying, for now. "I should go back to my farm soon. I haven't been there for months."

"We're all too busy now, Cherish. I can't see Levi letting you go when he's getting everyone to work in the orchard now. Even Hope has to give up her job.

He's not going to force Hope to quit and then let you go off on vacation."

Cherish sighed quietly. She wasn't going there for a vacation. It was hard work checking on everything Malachi had done, and on everything he'd decided without her say so. "I guess you're right. I'll have to wait a few months until the wintertime. Hopefully he won't do too much harm in that time."

"Who, Malachi?"

"*Jah.*"

"I'm sure he's capable. He's the bishop's nephew, isn't he?"

"*Jah.*"

"And, he recommended him, *jah?*"

"Correct."

"Well, then … why do you keep doubting him?"

"I don't know."

Joy laughed. "I can't blame you for anything you do or say anymore. Not when I burst into tears for nothing."

"You can blame me for anything if it makes you happy. It's okay. I'm used to it."

"You do get into a lot of trouble."

"That's all in the past. I'm growing up now and trying to be a much nicer person and be better behaved."

Joy glanced over at her again. "You already are a nice person. The best."

"*Denke,* Joy."

"I'm sure *Mamm* will take you to the farm when you go back."

"Take me there … you mean, like, go with me?"

"*Jah,* like Florence and Carter used to."

"That's right. They have Iris now. They probably won't drive me there ever again."

"*Mamm* will most likely hire a car like when you used to go to Aunt Dagmar's."

"Maybe." Cherish didn't think that was likely since she'd have to get Levi's approval. Drivers and hired cars didn't come cheap. She looked out the window again, and this time she was smiling as she remembered how she and Dagmar didn't get along at first. They were always butting heads about something. Now, Dagmar was the dearest person to her, next to her father. She was pleased she had been there at the farm the day Dagmar had died, and she was the last person to see her. That meant something, and she was sure Dagmar would've been pleased about it too.

"HERE WE ARE," said Joy when a small house came into their view.

"Not too bad at all." Cherish knew the inside would be much worse.

CHAPTER EIGHT

*B*liss liked nothing more than helping her stepmother in the kitchen. She missed her own mother so, and it was lovely to have the attention from Wilma when the two of them had their sleeves rolled up, talking about nothing in particular while they baked.

"When you've put that last pie in the oven, would you go to the mailbox and collect the mail? I'm expecting a letter from one of my cousins."

"Sure. When I come back, what will we do next?" Bliss hoped Wilma would keep working. Oftentimes when her father wasn't there, Wilma would sit in the living room and do nothing rather than keep working.

"Get the letters and that will give me time to think about it."

"Okay." Bliss put the last pie into the oven, and then wiped her hands on the hand towel that was kept by the sink before she walked out the back door. As she strolled down the driveway, she rolled the small white pebbles underneath her boots.

When giggling rang through the air, she looked up. It was coming from the shop. As she approached, the laughing got louder.

It didn't sound like Favor and Caroline were getting much work done. There were no customers, so they would've been being lazy, surely. Even with no customers there was still dusting, cleaning and making sure that all the packages and jars were straight.

Bliss poked her head through the doorway. "What's going on?"

They were both staring out the window at the road. They jumped and turned around when she spoke.

"Nothing," Caroline said sheepishly.

"I could hear you laughing from the *haus*."

"That's okay as long as *Mamm* didn't hear it," Favor said.

Bliss had noticed that Favor had changed since Caroline's visit. She was bolder, cheekier, and had a don't-care attitude. Surely *Mamm* and *Dat* could see that too? Why hadn't they sent Caroline home well before now? "I don't think so."

"I hope you haven't come to help us because as you can see, there's not much that needs to be done."

"Did you put the signs up at the crossroads?" Bliss asked.

They looked at one another. Favor shook her head. "We forgot."

Bliss crossed her arms over her chest. "That's not good. That's why you don't have any customers. They don't know we're open. Do it now before I tell *Dat*."

"*Nee*. You do it," Favor said.

"I can't. *Mamm* is expecting a letter and she wants me back right away so I can keep helping her in the kitchen. One of you can do it, and the other stay here in case we get customers."

"You're not the boss, Bliss."

"Well I'm older than you, so that does make me the boss."

"Only by a few months."

"That's close enough for me," said Bliss. "Actually, it's a year and a couple of months. I'm a whole year older than you."

Favor screwed up her nose. "It's such a long walk."

Bliss sighed. The family needed money from the shop and since neither of them wanted to do it, she knew she had to. "Favor, if you take the letters back to *Mamm*, I'll put the sign up."

"Don't trust her, she's up to something," said Caroline. "I'll put the signs out, just tell me where to do it."

Favor groaned. "It doesn't matter. I'll do it. You stay here, Caroline. It won't take me that long."

Caroline raised her hands in the air. "Where am I possibly going to go? The only place is to town and I'm not going near a horse. Hope has taken the only bike and I'm not walking all that way. I could hitchhike. As long as my parents don't hear about it. They'd have heart attacks."

Favor walked outside to get the signs that were leaning at the back of the store and Bliss walked with her to make sure she would do it.

"Don't you tell *Mamm* that I forgot to put the signs out."

"Of course I won't."

"*Denke*, Bliss."

Both girls walked down to the post box, which was a small white tin barrel below the sign that read Bakers Apple Orchard.

She opened it to see two letters. One addressed to her stepmother and one to Cherish.

Favor looked over her shoulder. "Oh, Cherish's got one. It must be from one of her pen pals."

"*Nee*, unless she has a man that is a pen pal."

"She doesn't; she would've said. Who's it from?"

"Malachi. This is her caretaker who's looking after her farm."

Favor sighed. "Nothing for me. I haven't been writing to my other pen pals much since Caroline's been here. She's been keeping me busy."

Bliss leaned against the signpost. "I heard Cherish mention him the other day. I think she said she hasn't heard from him or she was going to write to him. I wasn't really listening."

"Open it and see what it says," Favor said.

"I will not."

"We can glue it shut afterwards. That's exactly what Cherish would do to either of us."

"Nee! I'm surprised at you."

"Well, don't be. I decided that being good and following the rules doesn't really get anyone anywhere."

"It gets them into heaven. Do the right thing and you will be rewarded. With what measure you mete, it will be measured back to you," Bliss said.

Favor grabbed at the letter, but Bliss held it away from her. "C'mon Bliss. We can glue it back together."

"Aren't you listening, Favor?"

"Well … fine. But, you have a short memory."

Bliss frowned. "What do you mean?"

"Cherish wrote that letter to Adam Wengerd pretending to be you. Why don't you do the same? Write to this man pretending you're Cherish."

"Nee. When Cherish did that, it didn't end well for her. Do the right thing and you will be rewarded. Anyway, she confessed to me and said she was sorry. I forgave her so that's the end of the matter. You'd better hurry and put that sign out or I will tell *Mamm."*

"I'm going. Look how bad Cherish's been and she ends up getting everything she wants. Everyone likes her and I'm overlooked all the time."

"You are not. They allowed you to have Caroline stay. Now go put that sign out before *Dat* drives past and sees you've forgotten. He'll be upset. He's trying to make a big effort for the orchard and that includes the shop bringing in more money."

"I'll go." Favor walked off holding the heavy sign under her arm.

Bliss was tempted to help, but her stepmother was waiting on her and the letter. She walked back to the house. As she passed the shop again, she thought about Caroline. She wasn't a good influence on her stepsister. Couldn't her father and her stepmother see that?

Just as Bliss was about to step into the house, something caught her eye. She stopped, took a few paces back and looked up. It was one of her rabbits, one of the babies. It had gotten up to the window and it looked like it was sharpening its teeth on the wooden frame.

Wilma would never stop talking about it if she found out. She walked inside, breathed in the yummy aroma of the pies baking, and looked around for Wilma. Wilma was sitting down on the couch chewing something. She swallowed when she saw Bliss.

"There you are. Any letters?"

"Two letters, *Mamm*. One for you and the other for Cherish."

"Ah good. Make me a cup of hot tea, would you? I'll have a rest for a moment while I read the letter."

"Sure." Bliss filled the tea kettle with water, lit the stove and placed the kettle over it and then hurried upstairs.

"Wait, Bliss. What happened to my tea?"

By now Bliss was halfway up the stairs. "It's coming, *Mamm*. I'm just checking my rabbits while the water's boiling."

"*Ach!* Be sure to wash your hands after you've been touching those filthy beasts."

"I will." Bliss charged into her room and rabbits went scampering to and fro. Someone had opened the hutch. She quickly closed the door behind her so none would escape. Then, she walked over to the window to assess the damage. There was a large chunk out of one side of the wooden frame.

Wilma would notice it.

Somehow, she had to repair it before Wilma saw it. At least once a week Wilma looked at all their rooms to make sure they were keeping them spotless and tidy.

After she closed the rabbits away, she ran to the bathroom. What she needed was an enclosure so they could have more room to run about and be the lively rabbits that they were, but be unable to get into trouble.

Adam was making her one, he had said, but where was it? She'd remind him when she saw him next.

After giving her hands a thorough washing, she went back downstairs and made Wilma a cup of tea and put two chocolate cookies on a plate. When she placed them in front of Wilma, she didn't even notice it was there.

"*Mamm*, your tea."

"Ach, denke. Did you get one for yourself?"

"Nee." That was a sign that Wilma thought it was okay for her to have a break too. She sat down on the opposite couch.

Wilma put the letter down and reached for her tea.

"Finished the letter already, *Mamm?"*

"Nee. It's a long one this week."

"That's good. *Mamm,* can I ask you something?"

"Depends on what it is."

Bliss smiled. It was never a no or a yes with Wilma. "I would like an enclosure for the rabbits."

Wilma narrowed her eyes. *"Nee.* You have one already. What you have is big enough for one. One. I said you could keep one. All the others must go."

"But—"

"No buts. If you're going to annoy me with your endless talks about vermin, please go back to the kitchen and make sure those pies don't burn."

Bliss huffed.

"While you're doing that, peel the vegetables for tonight's evening meal. We're having visitors don't forget, so we'll need extra."

"Jah, Mamm." Bliss headed to the kitchen. It had been so long since Wilma had mentioned getting rid of the rabbits that she thought her stepmother was getting used to the idea of her keeping all the babies. The mother rabbit had now been taken to the vet, so there'd be no more babies, but then there were the baby ones and they were growing up quickly. She knew

her father wouldn't pay the money for all of them to have the same vet treatment. She'd have to find homes for them real soon.

As Bliss grabbed some potatoes, she knew what Wilma said was practical, but it would be so hard to see her babies leave home. And, how did she know they'd go to people who loved them as much as she did?

CHAPTER NINE

$\mathcal{C}$herish walked into Joy and Isaac's house eager to look around and get her first impression. The musty odor that enveloped her on opening the door had her stepping back before she knew what she was doing.

Joy looked at her with her hands on her hips. "What's wrong?"

"There is a terrible smell." She covered her nose. "I'm sorry, but it's true."

"I can't help that. It needs a good cleaning. That's why you're here helping, remember?"

"It's musty."

"That's probably the wood rot or the rising damp or the... The something. It's not so bad."

Cherish walked forward and went back inside. She could see Joy was enthusiastic and she didn't want to upset her or hurt her feelings. But something told her she might have already done that. She sniffed the air, twitching her nose like one of Bliss's bunnies. "Yeah, it's not that bad."

"It'll be gone soon."

"And is this where you'll be sleeping?" Cherish asked before she spun around the living room in a circle.

"*Jah*, this'll be our bedroom for now. Just for the next few days until they do the work on the place."

"Make them work on the bedrooms first."

"Isaac's doing that."

"Good idea. It must feel so good to be moving ahead with your life like this."

"It is. I don't know why I cried in the buggy just now. I am excited. Isaac is the best. Who knew that Christina would have such a good *bruder?*"

"Not me, that is for certain." Cherish looked around the room once more. "I can see that it won't take long to make it nice and then you've got about six months to live here with free rent, right?" Even though she'd already talked about that with Joy, she asked again. Surely there was some kind of a catch. It was odd that Levi was being so generous.

"That's right. I think so."

Cherish narrowed her eyes. She didn't like the uncertainty in her sister's voice. "What do you mean by, you think so?"

"I think that Levi will let us stay here for six

months after the baby's born. He wants to help us out."

"Interesting. Interesting that a man who is so mean with his money is suddenly being so generous."

"Oh, Cherish, he's not mean. He's just careful with his money and probably so that he'll have enough money to help people out when he wants to. Like helping out me and Isaac. "

"I'm sure you're right," Cherish said, even though she didn't believe it. Joy wasn't the one who had to hand over all her money when she worked outside the orchard like she and her sisters had to. At least she got to keep her tips that she squirreled away in secret. No one was going to touch those, but now Levi wanted her to leave the café all together. That would be hard. She loved working with the great variety of people that came and went. "I'll start bringing the kitchen things in, shall I?"

"Not yet. We have to clean the kitchen first."

"You mean, that's not been done yet?"

"No, come in and look at it. I thought that's why you were coming to help me today?"

"I am. How bad is it?"

"See for yourself." Joy showed Cherish the kitchen.

It was tiny. There was hardly any workspace, only one small sink and three small cupboards. "It's not too bad. You need a table in here for an extra working area."

"I know. Levi's bringing some furniture for us later today."

"Good. It just needs a good dusting and a good cleaning. I'd say it would be as good as new in a couple of hours. I'll go to the buggy and get the cleaning things."

"*Denke,* Cherish."

Cherish hurried out the door. She couldn't wait till she got back into the fresh air to get away from the closed-up stink of the house. She sniffed her sleeve hoping that she wouldn't come away smelling like the house. At least she was wearing her oldest dress and she'd boil it as soon as she got home. If that didn't work, she'd simply throw it out. She got the box of cleaning things out of the buggy, took them in the house and then made a second trip to get the broom and mop.

Once she was back inside, she opened all the doors and the windows.

When they were in the midst of cleaning the kitchen, Isaac arrived in the wagon, bringing with him two strong friends to help.

BY THE TIME they left the house that afternoon, the sun had gone down. Only its afterglow could still be seen on the horizon.

Cherish was exhausted.

Isaac and Joy drove Cherish back to the house and they were all more than ready for a big feed at the family dinner Wilma had organized.

CHAPTER TEN

*C*herish was disappointed her older half-brother, Mark and his wife Christina weren't there. They were family too. Why didn't Wilma make more of an effort to include them? As usual, *Mamm's* best friend Ada and her husband Samuel were there. They were always there for family dinners.

Tonight would be a good night to mention the will, Cherish thought once she sat around the large table. Everyone would be shocked, and what would Wilma have to say?

But she couldn't raise the subject. She'd promised. Keeping such a secret was eating away at Cherish. It had taken all her self-control not to tell Joy, to see what she thought about it.

Halfway through the meal, Levi cleared his throat loudly, the way he normally did when he had some-thing to say. Cherish looked over at him and then looked away when she saw him picking something out of his teeth.

A moment later, he cleared his throat even louder and a hush fell over the table. This time, he had his hands on the table, so it was safe to look at him.

When he looked over at Caroline, Cherish heaved a silent sigh. He wasn't going to complain about her. She was off the hook this time. Not that she could think of anything bad she'd done of late. Unless he knew about her snooping in her mother's things in their bedroom, but no one here knew about that.

"Caroline, now that things are more normal around here, we'll have to see about getting you a ticket back home. Your parents must miss you after all this time you've been away from them."

"Yes, I will organize it, Mr. Bruner. I don't want to outstay my welcome."

All eyes were now on Levi waiting for his response. Seconds went by without Levi opening his mouth.

Then it was up to Wilma to speak. "You won't outstay your welcome. We're worried that your parents will miss you and surely … don't you have college?"

"I'm on break. I can always catch up online if I miss some classes. It's under control."

"Oh." Wilma looked down at the table and didn't say any more.

Now Cherish looked at the food in front of her and she could feel the tension emanating from Favor. She was dreadfully upset that Caroline would have to go home, but her pen pal had been there long enough. And if Favor was upset, Caroline would be too. For some reason that Cherish couldn't figure out, Caroline didn't want to go home.

"She's not outstayed her welcome," Favor said.

Again, everyone looked at Levi expecting him to say that she wasn't outstaying her welcome, but he said nothing at all.

It was obvious Caroline liked Hope's boyfriend, Fairfax, the way she kept staring at him across the dinner table. When she wasn't staring at Fairfax, she was looking at Adam. Both were handsome men.

"You do have to get back though, don't you?" Ada asked. "I mean, you can't stay here forever."

Favor's lips turned down at the corners and Cherish was surprised that Ada was getting involved. After all, it was none of her business.

"I know. I'll organize something tomorrow. I want to thank you, Mr. and Mrs. Bruner, for having me here. It's been … well, it's been the most enjoyable time of my life."

"Has it?" Wilma asked. "What's your home like?"

"My folks work all the time. I hardly see them. It's not very nice to come home to an empty house. Your house is never empty and it's full of so much life."

Ada smiled. "Surely you have friends?"

"I do have some friends, but I'm not in any great hurry to get home."

All Levi did with that news was raise his bushy

eyebrows. It seemed a bit rude, but sometimes that was how Levi acted.

"She can come again, though, can't she?" Favor asked.

After Levi didn't respond, Wilma said, *"Jah,* that would be fine."

"By the time you come back, Caroline, our house should be all fixed up," Joy said. "And I would've had the *boppli."*

"I can't wait to see them both."

"By that time, Joy, you and Isaac will be out of there and into your own home," Ada said.

"Ach, even better," Joy said with a smile.

"You need some help over at the *haus?"* Fairfax asked Isaac.

"I will next week if you can spare some time."

"I'll be there."

Samuel said, "What about your work on the dairy, Fairfax?"

"I have hours during the daytime where I can help. I'm sure the Millers' will understand. I mainly help them with fixing fences and doing odd jobs during the day, but if they know I'll be helping someone they'll be okay."

"Ah, good. Just didn't want you walking out on your work."

"He'd never do that," Hope told Samuel.

Samuel smiled and raised his hands. "Okay."

Timmy, the budgie, whistled as though he was mimicking 'okay.'

Everyone laughed when Timmy kept repeating it. Everyone, except Wilma.

"Quiet that bird, Cherish. We shouldn't have to put up with that noise when we're trying to eat. Put it on the porch."

"*Nee*. I can't do that. He hates being outside. I put him outside once and other birds came and tormented him. I'll just put the cover over him."

"If it doesn't stop its noise, my next meal will be bird pie."

"That's not funny," Bliss said to Wilma. "Please don't talk about him like that."

All eyes were on Bliss, surprised to hear her speaking to her stepmother like that. Bliss's words had been sharp but she'd still said them most politely.

"Bliss!" Ada said.

"I'm sorry, *Mamm*, but you're always making jokes about rabbit stew, too. And I don't find it funny when you're talking about eating our pets that we love very much."

Cherish put the cover over Timmy. "That's right. It's not funny." She couldn't let Bliss go out on a limb like that all on her own. She had to back her up.

"Stop it now all of you," Ada said with her voice raised.

"Why can't we just have a nice family dinner without having arguments and animals? It's always about animals. I've a good mind to get rid of them all," Wilma said.

"Except the horses," Levi was quick to add. He loved his horses.

Cherish sat back down. *"Mamm,* we wouldn't have to say such things if you would just stop making jokes about making rabbit or budgie pie."

"I said *bird* pie."

"Same difference."

Ada interrupted again, "You're carrying on the argument, Cherish."

Cherish sat there in silence. Again, it had all become her fault. Now would be an excellent time to raise the subject of the will. A smile raised the edges of Cherish's lips.

"Let's talk about something happy then, shall we?" Caroline said.

"And what would be happy to a girl like you, Caroline?" Ada asked.

"Joy having a baby, that's very exciting. I can't wait for the day when that happens for me. I'll have plenty of nannies and a housekeeper, and when they get older, someone to drive them to and from school, to their sporting events. I'd have it all worked out."

"Wouldn't you want to do all those things yourself?" Ada asked.

"No. I'd be concentrating on getting my figure back. I do have a certain look to maintain." She stared at Fairfax from under her long dark lashes.

"You're not fat," said Hope.

"And that's how it'll stay."

"At last that silly bird's quiet," Wilma said. "Dessert! It's time for dessert."

Ada stood to help Wilma carry the desserts to the table while Hope and Cherish cleared the table of the items from the main meal.

As they did so, Cherish heard Wilma whispering to Ada, "These animals will be the death of me."

Ada replied, "Just get rid of them. Say the bird got away while you were cleaning the cage."

Cherish put the pile of plates loudly on the kitchen counter. "I heard that. And, if that happens, I'll never talk to either of you again. I will leave this house and never come back. What's more, I'll reveal all of your secrets." She pointed at Wilma. "Don't touch my bird!" Cherish was so angry, she felt she might faint. The bird would die if they let him out. He wouldn't know how to live in the wild.

Levi jumped out of his chair and hurried over. "What's going on?"

CHAPTER ELEVEN

"*I* was just having a private joke with Wilma, and Cherish thought we were serious," Ada said.

"I'd never do that, Cherish," Wilma said with her bottom lip wobbling. "Don't be upset."

"What is this about and why would you mention secrets, Cherish?" Levi asked.

Cherish felt sick to the stomach. "I'll be in my room. Alone. Please, everyone leave me be." Cherish hurried out of the room and ran up the stairs to her bedroom.

While she was looking out the window counting the days until she could leave the place, Hope walked into her room. "This is so embarrassing for me. Can't you see that, Cherish? Fairfax might think all the families in the community are like ours, fighting and arguing all the time. It's just not normal. Why can't we just have a normal family?"

"He's staying at the Millers.' They're normal, so it's hardly a worry."

Hope slumped onto Cherish's bed. "Can't you just set a good example? Come down and apologize to *Mamm* for the outburst?"

"Do you know what she said? It was actually Ada who said it, but *Mamm* might've done it. I don't trust her anymore—either of them."

"I know, but can you see things from my point of view? It's not how a family should behave."

Cherish sighed. "You're right. I'll do it for you." Cherish leaned over and hugged Hope. "I'll do it for Fairfax too. I've always gotten along with him."

"*Denke.* Let's go."

"I'll say the words of apology for my part of what happened, but in my heart, nothing will change."

Hope nodded. "That'll have to do."

They walked back down the stairs together. Cherish stood in the kitchen and everyone stopped talking and looked over their desserts at her. "I'm sorry for my outburst. It will not happen again."

"All is forgiven and forgotten," Levi said. "Sit down and your *mudder* will get you a dessert plate."

Cherish sat down and then Wilma rose up from the table and put a dessert plate in front of her. Cherish knew Wilma wasn't happy.

As Wilma sat down, she said, "Cherish, before I forget, there's a letter for you. It arrived today."

"A letter for me?"

"*Jah*, it's from Malachi."

"He's finally written. Where is it?"

"You'll get it when you finish tonight's cleaning up and not a moment before."

"It's not Cherish's turn tonight," Bliss said.

"The more people helping the quicker it will get through," Ada said.

Cherish ate her apple pie and cream not even listening to the conversation that tried to invade her ears.

When the guests finished and headed to the living room, Cherish stayed in the kitchen with Favor and Caroline to help with the washing and drying up.

"Who is Malachi, Cherish?" asked Caroline, while she and Cherish cleared the table.

"He's the caretaker of my farm. He never does what he's told, but he does seem to be doing a reasonable job even if he's doing things that I wouldn't do."

"You can't complain about that, then."

"Ah, but Cherish likes to complain," Favor said.

Mamm entered the room and added, "She's happy when she's complaining."

Cherish's mouth fell open at *Mamm's* words. "That's not so, that's not so at all. I only complain when I see something wrong or hear something wrong." She wanted to say, 'Like that will of *Dat's* you've got hidden

83

in your closet,' but she managed to restrain herself. She had given Carter her word that she'd keep quiet about it until he and Florence figured out what to do.

"I have heard you complain a lot since I've been here," Caroline teased her.

"Well who is doing the complaining now? You're all complaining right now about me complaining, and so are you, *Mamm.*"

Wilma smiled. "I wouldn't say so." Wilma waved the letter from Malachi in her outstretched hand.

"I can't open it, *Mamm*. It could be bad news. Something terrible could've happened."

"If it had, I'm sure he would've called our phone in the barn. I'll put the letter here and you can read it when you finish this work." Wilma busied herself filling up the teakettle.

As Cherish stacked the dishes ready for one of the others to wash, she wondered how everybody would react when they heard about the will. Wilma would deny knowledge of it and go to bed with one of her imaginary headaches. Joy would tell everyone to pray about it and everything will turn out fine. It wouldn't affect Mercy and Honor, the older two sisters, because they were too busy with their own families now and didn't even live in the area. Favor wouldn't care because she would still have her pen pals—the only thing she seemed to care about. Bliss would worry about how it would affect her rabbits, and Hope would think it was all a bad example for Fairfax.

Wilma took out their largest teapot and shook in some tea leaves without even using a spoon. Cherish had been taught it was one spoon of tea leaves for each person and one for the pot. Now it seemed Wilma wasn't even following her own rules.

As Cherish picked up the last dinner plate from the table, she looked around the corner into the living room and saw Levi talking with Samuel. What would he think about his wife keeping a secret from him? He would have to wonder whether she would do the same when he died. Perhaps he would want to leave most things to Bliss, and what would happen if Wilma kept his will a secret from Bliss and kept it all for herself? There was no doubt in Cherish's mind Levi would not trust Wilma when he found out the truth.

"Hurry up, Cherish. You can dry while Caroline and I take turns washing the dishes." Cherish turned and took a step, but then her foot caught and she landed on the floor, and the plate dropped from her hands and smashed onto the floor. Pieces of white dinner plate went everywhere. Then something scampered out of the kitchen.

Wilma ran to her. "Cherish, are you all right?"

Cherish pulled herself up into a seated position. "I think I'm okay."

Everyone ran into the kitchen and stared at Cherish.

"It was a rabbit! This is the last straw of the last straw. Bliss, take your rabbits to your room and I'm selling them at the markets tomorrow," *Mamm* called out.

"You can't do that. They're mine."

"Don't speak back," Levi warned his daughter.

Bliss managed to corner the scared rabbit, and then took hold of him and hurried over the broken pieces of china, past everyone and ran up to her bedroom.

Caroline and Favor were quick to collect the broken pieces and sweep up the small shards.

Cherish said, "There's really no problem, *Mamm*, I'm okay. Nothing is broken. The rabbit just got out of his hutch somehow."

Wilma shook her head as Isaac stepped forward and helped Cherish to her feet.

"I've been too nice for too long," Wilma said.

"About what?" Hope asked.

"About Bliss and those rabbits. I told her she could only have one and now that one multiplied and she still hasn't gotten rid of the babies."

"They're not babies anymore, they're nearly full-grown," said Favor, not helping the situation at all.

Cherish was glad no one thought to mention that the 'babies' would soon be old enough to start their own multiplying.

"We'll go now," Ada said, poking her head around the corner. "*Denke* for a *wunderbaar* dinner, Wilma, but it's getting late."

"Oh, you don't normally go this early."

"I'll have to go too, Mrs. Bruner. The cows … need milking early," Fairfax said.

"Fine. I understand you have an early start."

Joy said, "Isaac and I have had a big day. We'll go too." Joy ran over and kissed her mother on the cheek, and then turned and hurried out of the house with Isaac.

Once all the guests left, one after the other, Wilma announced, "The night is ruined." *Mamm* marched out of the kitchen.

Cherish, Hope, and the other girls listened at the kitchen door while *Mamm* complained to Levi about all the rabbits in the house.

CHAPTER TWELVE

"*C*an't you understand that this is an orchard? Any orchard or any place with large dogs cannot abide rabbits," Wilma told Levi.

"They are pet rabbits," Bliss yelled out from the top of the stairs.

"I'm talking to your father, I'm not talking to you," Wilma called back.

"Someone's opening the hutch and getting me into trouble. It's happened more than once now."

Levi said, "Go back into your room, Bliss." A few seconds later, after they all heard the loud closing of a door. "It will break her heart if she has no rabbits, Wilma. Let her keep her original rabbit and I'm sure she'll be able to find homes for the others."

"That's what she said she's been doing. She tells me she can't find homes."

"Here's what I'd do. Charge each girl with one

rabbit to sell or give away. As I heard you say just now in the kitchen, when everyone shares the workload things get done much quicker."

"It was Ada who said that. But it *is* a good idea. Involve the girls. I'm glad I married you."

Cherish made a face as the lovey-dovey talk turned her stomach. She looked around the corner and saw them smiling at one another. She hurried back to the sink when she saw Wilma stand up.

When Wilma walked into the kitchen, she announced, "Each of you will have one rabbit that you'll have to get rid of. I don't care how you get rid of it, just get rid of it."

"*Mamm,* they'd have to go to a good home," said Cherish. "That should be your main concern. For Bliss's sake."

"Very well, Cherish. You're a very kind girl. Each of you shouldn't have a problem with only one rabbit to find a home for."

"How are we supposed to do that?" asked Favor. "We only know people that Bliss has probably already asked."

Wilma threw her hands in the air. "That's your problem to figure out, not mine. You could go door-to-door."

"Knock on strangers' doors?" Favor gulped.

"*Jah.*"

Caroline said, "We could do that tomorrow, Favor. It'll be fun."

"I'll take my rabbit to work. Maybe a family will come in and fall in love with it," Hope said.

Cherish rolled her eyes while wondering how she could offload the rabbit she'd be given and whether it was *Mamm* who kept opening the hutch and letting the rabbits escape. That way she would get Levi onside to help pressure Bliss to get rid of the rabbits. It was something *Mamm* would do. Then Cherish remembered her letter from Malachi. She still hadn't opened it.

"I'll not be around for much longer. I'll have to buy my ticket tomorrow."

"There must be another way," Favor whispered to Caroline.

CHAPTER THIRTEEN

*F*lorence was still worried about doing the right thing. She didn't want to upset Wilma and Levi, but at the same time, she wanted what was supposed to be hers. Carter had one opinion and she had another.

Earl! Her big brother would be able to give her advice. With Carter upstairs trying to get Iris to sleep, Florence picked up her cell phone. She called Earl, praying he'd hear the phone in the barn and be close enough to answer it. It was just before nine, so this was her best chance of contacting him.

"Hello?"

She heaved a relieved sigh at the sound of his voice. "Earl."

"Hello Florence, I haven't heard from you in a while. How are Iris and Carter?"

"Good, good. They're doing just fine."

"Is everything all right? You don't often call just to talk. You only call when you have news. Otherwise you write."

"Everything's okay, nothing to worry about, but I had surprising news from Cherish the other day."

He chuckled. "What's that girl up to now?"

"It's nothing that she did. She came here with something she found when she was looking in Wilma's bedroom. It's a will and … it's *Dat's* will."

"Is that right?"

"Yes."

"He told me he had a will. When he died, Wilma couldn't find it. I'm glad she's found it."

That supported the fact that Wilma was concealing it. "Wilma doesn't know Cherish found it."

"What are you saying?"

"Cherish had doubts about the orchard's ownership and thought that Levi might own it now. She was snooping in *Mamm's* room when she came across it."

There was silence at the other end.

Florence recalled his earlier words. "So, you knew that there was a will?"

"*Jah. Dat* talked about it with me and with Mark."

"I never knew any conversations took place. You see, he named Wilma as the executor, and doesn't that mean she's supposed to see that things are carried out properly?"

"I'm sure that's what it means."

"Carter took a copy of it and I … I just don't know

what to do. We told Cherish to put it back where she found it." She lowered her voice. "Carter says to forget it, but what about what *Dat* wanted?"

"All I know is he asked me and Mark about it. We said we didn't want the orchard. He was pleased to leave it to you. He said you were just as devoted to it as he was."

"What else did he say?" Again, there was silence. "Come on, tell me what else he said."

"He said he knew you'd never leave the trees. He knew Mark and I would, the first chance we got."

Florence was disappointed in herself for leaving the orchard. If she'd stayed, Wilma probably never would've married Levi. Maybe if she'd stayed, Wilma would've produced the will—eventually—and her father's will could've been acted upon officially.

"Look, Florence, the orchard and the trees, as pretty as they might be and all that, are just a means to an end to give the family an income. That's why *Dat* wanted you to keep running it because he knew you were sensible and would do the right thing by everybody. He trusted you to look after everyone."

She sighed when she thought about how she'd walked away and left everything be with Carter. "That's where I'm confused, Earl. What is the right thing to do now? Now that Wilma is married to Levi? What do you think?"

"Well…"

"You see, I'm in two minds. If I thought Levi and

Wilma were going to live there forever that would be okay. I would walk away and forget it, but he's been talking about selling. So, what if he sells and *Dat's* orchard goes to someone else? *Dat* would want it to stay in the family."

"You're right about that."

"And I've offered to buy the farm—Carter and I have, but he's not interested in selling to us. Do you see my problem?"

"I do and it sounds like a problem with no easy solution. You will have to think on it and pray on it.'"

"Don't you have any advice to give me?"

"*Nee.* I wouldn't like to be in your place. There are too many fors and againsts with no easy solution. If you make known the contents or even the existence of the will, what will be the impact on Wilma?"

"I've been thinking about that, but then I realize she wasn't caring about me when she hid it."

"If you raise the subject of the will, then what would be the next step?"

"I'm hoping to use it as leverage for them to sell to me. And of course I'd carry out the rest of his wishes that everyone always has a home in the house. Any one of the family who wants to live there, well, they can. Carter and I will just continue living where we are now. The girls told me Levi's not doing a good job of running the orchard."

"They shouldn't be telling stories like that. You should've taught them better."

"It's not easy. When *Dat* died and you and Mark left, Wilma fell in a heap and it was left for me to do everything." Didn't Earl see that? How could he say she should've taught them better? She wasn't their mother, even so, she couldn't do more than she'd already done.

"I know you were stuck with everything."

"I'm shocked you would say that to me about teaching them better. I did the best I could." At that moment, Carter walked down the stairs frowning curiously, trying to work out who she was talking with. She mouthed the word 'Earl' and he nodded, before he headed into the kitchen.

"It's late, Florence, I've an early start in the morning. I don't know what to advise you to do. I'll help you pray about it."

"Thanks." Then Florence heard him hang up the receiver. She ended the call on her screen and tossed the phone onto the couch. No one seemed to be in her corner, and no one had an easy answer. Carter had said he'd back her up, but she knew he was doing it reluctantly. His heart wasn't in it.

Wilma has caused this problem, she thought. *I need to speak with her and sort this out.*

CHAPTER FOURTEEN

*C*herish finished up in the kitchen and then grabbed the letter that Wilma had perched on the edge of the countertop.

She ripped it open, pulled out the letter, and then sat down at the newly wiped-down kitchen table to read.

While she was sitting there quietly, Hope came into the kitchen, grabbed a glass and filled it with water.

"Hey, Hope, listen to this. This is what Malachi says in his letter. 'I miss your visits, and our talks. When are you going to visit again?' What do you think he means by that? Do you think he likes me? Because I don't want him getting the wrong idea. I could never be interested in someone like him. I mean, look at how he writes—all messy—and he doesn't talk properly. He uses all the wrong words. We don't even get along that well."

Hope swallowed a mouthful of water and then sat down with Cherish. "I don't know. Why don't you ask someone with more experience with men? I've only ever been interested in one man and that's Fairfax. I don't know anything, not really. To me, it sounds like he could like you but only as a friend. The farm is isolated and he could be lonely and hoping you'll visit again. It has been a while since you've been there."

Cherish knew she couldn't ask her mother because *Mamm* didn't know what she was doing with men or she wouldn't have married a man like Levi. If she followed *Mamm's* advice, surely she'd end up making many wrong choices in life. "Who would I possibly ask?"

"I'm not sure."

"Caroline! She'd know. *Denke.* I'll ask her."

Hope moved her glass around on the table. "I didn't say Caroline."

"I know. It was my idea to ask her. She's good with men. I've seen how she talks to them at the meetings and things. They all smile at her. She'll tell me what to say so Malachi doesn't get the wrong idea."

"Just to be clear, in case this whole thing goes wrong in some way, I didn't say to ask Caroline."

"What could possibly go wrong?"

"I don't even want to think about that, but if you think she can help, ask her if you want."

"I will."

Joy and Isaac walked into the kitchen.

"Hey, I thought you two had left already," Cherish said.

"*Nee,* I had to make a trip to the bathroom again," Joy said, while Isaac fetched her a glass of water.

"*Jah,*" Isaac said, "we had to turn around and come back."

"Are you sure you'll be okay in that house of Levi's?" Cherish asked them.

"*Jah,*" Joy said. "The men have blocked off the bad rooms for now."

"Ugh. I can't imagine anyone living there. Levi said he had people renting it, before, but how did they live in it?"

Isaac handed the glass to Joy. "It'll be fixed by the time the baby arrives and it'll allow us more time to save more money."

Joy drank the water in double-quick time.

Hope put her hand out to take the glass. "I'll put it in the sink for you."

"*Denke. Gut nacht,* all. Oh! I think the *boppli* just kicked."

"Really? Can I feel it?" Isaac moved to touch her belly.

"No. No, I don't think it was. It was a flutter. It might've been my imagination."

Hope groaned. "I wish I was having a *boppli.*"

"You'd be in a spot of trouble if you were," Joy said with a laugh.

"Well, not from *Mamm* because—" blurted Cherish.

Joy interrupted her with a glare. "Hush, Cherish. No one is to know about that."

"A lot of people know."

"Don't speak a word about it," Joy snapped at her while Isaac stood there looking displeased with Cherish, but not saying a word.

Cherish sighed. "Okay. That's another thing to add to my list of dos and don'ts. I wish I could live a normal life without worrying that I'll upset someone. People should really be worrying that they'll upset me, but no one cares about that."

"*Gut nacht,*" Isaac said over his shoulder while ushering his wife out the door.

"Good night," Cherish and Hope said at the same time, just before the newly married couple vanished.

Cherish smoothed down her letter. "It must be awful to have to watch how much you spend. It's taking such a long time for them to save for a place of their own. I feel for them."

"They'll get there. We can't all be given a *haus* free and clear like you," Hope said with a snigger.

Cherish knew her sister wasn't saying that out of jealousy. Hope was happy for her. "A farm, not just a *haus*. I'll forever be grateful to Aunt Dagmar. We were so close. It was like she was my *mudder*. I was closer to her than *Mamm*."

"Oh, don't tell *Mamm* that. She'll be upset."

"It's a fact."

"*Jah,* but still. Those things can hurt people. Cut

like a knife." Hope made a sawing motion with the side of her hand against her arm.

"Facts can hurt?"

"Words."

"Life is so odd, isn't it? Don't tell lies, but don't tell facts either. Facts are truths and you're supposed to tell the truth, but not if someone will be upset, or if you're revealing a secret. Nothing seems black or white and that's why life can get confusing."

"It's regarding someone else's feelings, that's all. You are so dramatic sometimes. It's not that hard."

"It is for me."

Hope looked at Cherish's letter. "Can I read it?"

Cherish didn't want anyone reading her letter, but couldn't think of a reason why. "Okay." She handed it over and sat there watching Hope's face as she read it.

"Ah, I see what you mean. It's hard to figure out what he's saying at all. His spelling is not good and his handwriting is worse."

"I know. I couldn't possibly be interested in him."

Hope leaned forward. *"Jah,* you said that, but what if he likes you? You want to nip that in the bud before he gets his feelings hurt."

"I don't want that. I think he's basically nice. We could be friends under different circumstances." Cherish sighed as she snatched back the letter. "I'll take it to Caroline now and see what she thinks."

"They'll still be awake. They stay up late talking and giggling."

"I know." Cherish left Hope in the kitchen and headed up the stairs.

When she got to Favor's door, she heard them talking. She put her ear against the door in case they were talking about her.

CHAPTER FIFTEEN

ith Cherish's ear pressed up against the bedroom door where Caroline was staying with Favor, she listened hard.

"Did you hear what your father said about me going home? I don't want to. I'm not ready to go back. My folks don't care how long I stay. They said it was doing me good."

"Why don't we change Levi's mind?"

Cherish was shocked by Favor's words.

"By the way, he's not my father," Favor added.

"I know. He's your stepfather."

"That's right. You want to stay and I want you to stay, right?"

"Yes."

Favor said, "Lately, I've been living my life by thinking of what Cherish would do. She always gets her way. She might get into trouble, but in the end, she's always better off for being tricky. So, what would make Levi be happy for you to stay, want you to stay even?"

Cherish could barely hide the smile when she heard that Favor wanted to be like her.

"Um … if he thought I was in some kind of danger he'd surely want me to stay here. I mean, that would be the decent thing to do."

"Yes. That's it, Caroline. That's it. You have to be in danger if you go back. I mean, Levi and *Mamm* have to believe you'll be in danger."

Unbelievable! I'd never do anything like this, Cherish thought.

"What if I told him … my house burned down, and my parents are staying with my grandparents and there's no room for me? Nowhere for me to live. I'd be homeless."

Favor giggled. "I don't know. That's a lie. Has your house burned down?"

"You know it hasn't."

"I wouldn't be comfortable with telling him that."

It was an outright lie and Cherish was shocked.

"You want me to go home, Favor?" Caroline whimpered.

"No, I want you to stay."

"He's going to send me home if we don't do something. I love it here. I just want to stay a little bit longer. It's been good, me staying here."

"Levi wasn't happy about that video that went out."

"It ended up okay. Levi even talked to that reporter."

"Yeah, that was a surprise. He wasn't happy about what you did, though."

"That's in the past. I said I was sorry and it all worked out in the end. You won't have to lie if you're so goody-goody about it. I'll tell him about the house burning down. I'll ask him if I can stay just another week. Surely he won't turn me out on the street."

"Okay, and you are a good helper in the kitchen. *Mamm* will want you to stay."

"Do you think so?"

"Yes. She likes you a lot."

"Good. I'd really like to know how your *Mamm* makes apple pies so delicious. They're so much better than store-bought. I'll ask if she can show me."

Cherish burst through the door. "I heard everything. All your schemes and plans."

Both girls looked at her with their mouths gaping open.

Caroline was the first to speak. "Cherish, will you keep my secret?"

She hadn't expected a soft approach from Caroline and it took her by surprise. She closed the door behind her and thought through her answer before she spoke. "I can't make any promises. I don't think it's a good idea. You'll be found out and how will you feel about that?"

"You always get away with it," Favor blurted out.

"I do not."

"Do too."

"I'm always in my room for opening my mouth about something."

"Just keep the secret for now, will you? At least so I can stay another week. I really have an awful life back home."

Cherish knew that wasn't true. Caroline lived a privileged life and didn't lack one thing. From what she'd said, her parents had more money than they knew what to do with.

Folding her arms in front of her, Cherish stared at Caroline and tried to work her out. What made her want to stay in a place where she had to work when she could go home and do nothing? There was more to it, and Cherish already knew what it was. "I feel so sorry for you if your life is so bad. Sure, I'll keep quiet. When you're telling Levi about the house fire, be sure to cry."

"Oh, I will. I've always found that to work."

"How are you going to make yourself cry?" Favor asked.

"I'll just think of something sad."

"And that works?"

"Yes."

"What will you think of?" asked Cherish.

"One week I didn't get my allowance because I accidentally borrowed my mom's car. It was so unjust."

Favor frowned. "That's awful. You're not allowed to drive it?"

"I was twelve at the time."

Cherish could barely stop her lips from forming a smile. "'Accidentally borrowed' it, hmm?"

"The point is, I didn't get my allowance. They could've yelled at me and it would've been done. It was so mean to take my allowance from me. I needed it to play an online computer game with my friends. You have to pay money to do that."

"When are you going to talk to Levi?" Cherish asked, trying to move the conversation along. She still hadn't gotten around to the reason she'd come to their bedroom.

"Tomorrow. I'm allowed to turn my cell phone on when I'm not in the house. I'll go for a walk and then my folks can give me the dreadful news."

Cherish folded her arms. "And what reason will you give them for not coming home?"

"I'll say someone has fallen ill and I'm staying to help out. Maybe someone could fall off a ladder and break their leg. They'll be pleased about me helping with that. They're always trying to make me do charity work for the poor and the homeless, and that'll be the same kind of thing."

"We're not poor," Cherish said with her nose in the air.

"My folks don't know that."

Cherish made a face. Even so, she didn't like Caroline's parents thinking she had to help them because one of them was ill, or they were poor, or someone had a broken leg.

Favor stared at Cherish. "Do you have a better idea?"

"Keep me out of it. When it all comes crashing down, I'm going to be far, far away. This'll be one thing they can't blame on me." She pulled out the letter and handed it to Caroline. "I need your advice."

Caroline read through the letter with Favor looking over her shoulder.

Cherish made herself comfortable on the floor.

Caroline looked up and handed the letter back. "What advice do you want?"

"Does he like me? Look at his words about missing me and stuff."

"Very much so. Can't you tell that?"

"Ach nee." Cherish ripped the letter in two. "This is dreadful."

"I said he *does* like you."

"Cherish doesn't want him to like her. He's just not suitable and she doesn't want to cause problems. She needs him to stay there until she takes over the place. She put the word out for a caretaker and he was the only one interested."

"He'll stay because he likes you."

Cherish sighed. Caroline just didn't understand how bad this was. When he found out she didn't like him, he could leave. Then who would look after her farm?

CHAPTER SIXTEEN

The next morning, Bliss was crying as each of the girls was handed a rabbit and instructed by Wilma to find a home for it. "I expect them to be gone by nightfall," Wilma told them.

"Make sure they're good homes," Bliss said through her tears.

"They will do their best, Bliss. I've already made this clear to you."

"I know, but I want the new owners to treat them well. I've treated them well and now I just want them to go to good homes."

"Each of the girls told us they would find them good new homes."

"How am I supposed to make sure that happens when I've got to be working in the shop today?"

Wilma sighed. "Bliss, you had plenty of time. I gave

you plenty of time to find homes and you haven't found one. I had to do something."

"It's not going to be easy."

"Nothing is when you have that attitude." Wilma fixed her hands on her hips and stared at Bliss.

"Okay I'll do my best not to worry."

Hope gave her rabbit back to Bliss. "Hold onto him for a while. I'll just have to ask everybody who comes into the Bed and Breakfast if they want a rabbit."

"As a pet," Bliss said.

"Yes, of course for a pet. Maybe some children will come in and want a nice fluffy bunny."

"I hope so."

"If you're opening the store, Cherish, you'd better go now."

"Okay, I'm going."

"The girls will help you carry the boxes."

Hope, Caroline and Favor helped her carry newly baked apple pies to the shop. Cherish unlocked the door and walked in and as soon as the girls dumped the boxes on the countertop they all disappeared, including Hope who said she was going to make an early start.

The first thing Cherish did was make a sign to stick to the wall.

"One rabbit to give away to a good home."

She crumpled up that bit of paper and threw it away. Then she took out a fresh sheet of paper.

"One baby rabbit to give away to a good home."

She didn't want them to think they were getting an old rabbit. Then she had an idea. *Why not put an ad in the paper?*

Daniel worked at the paper, and surely this was a legitimate reason to contact him.

As soon as Favor and Caroline got back from their unsuccessful rabbit-giving-away trip a couple of hours later, Cherish had them look after the store while she ran to the barn.

She flipped open the phone book and found the number of the local English newspaper where Daniel worked. She called them and told them she had something interesting to tell their reporter. They soon gave her Daniel's cell phone number which she scribbled down in the phone book her family wrote all their numbers in.

She called him, and waited in anticipation with a fast-beating heart. When he answered, she said, "Daniel, this is Cherish Baker from—"

"Cherish Baker from the apple orchard."

"That's right. You remember me."

"That's right. Are you calling me to ask when the story will be coming out in the paper?"

"No not really."

"I expect it'll be coming out next week. As soon as I can get it approved. The editor has been so busy with all the political happenings that are going on right now. It's really quite stressful."

"I know what you mean," Cherish said. "What I'm calling about is … I have a rabbit I need to give away. I need to put an advertisement in your paper."

"You'll have to call someone else about that. I have nothing to do with the ads."

"Don't you? But you work at the paper."

He laughed. "I don't work on that section. I can give you the number of it. Or you can come to the newspaper office."

"Where you work?"

"That's right. How about you come down tomorrow and, after you fix the ad, I'll take you for a cup of coffee."

"Oh, I'd like that very much and … I think I'd be able to get away from the shop for a while."

"Excellent."

"Thank you. And how much is the ad likely to cost?"

"Not much, not very much at all. When you get here ask for me. I'll handle it personally from there."

Cherish gasped. "You'd do that?"

"I would."

Cherish was delighted. "I'll see you tomorrow then. I think I can get there about eleven."

"I'll be looking forward to it."

"Me too." Cherish hung up the phone's receiver.

Later that evening, Hope was able to tell everyone that she had found a lovely family to give one of the rabbits to. The family came to the house after dinner, and not only did they take one rabbit, they took two.

Even Bliss was smiling at the faces of the children as they held the rabbits.

CHAPTER SEVENTEEN

*T*he next day, it was just after eleven when Cherish arrived at the newspaper office. She asked to speak to Daniel and they offered to let her go through to his office but she said she would wait for him right there behind the counter. Minutes later, he appeared with a bright smile.

"Cherish, it's nice to see you again."

"And you."

"I know we said coffee, but would you have time to make it lunch?"

"For certain. We could go to the café where I work. They have good food."

"Sounds like a plan. Have you already written out the ad?"

Cherish had been so excited about their coffee date, she'd forgotten all about the job she had of giving away a rabbit, and the ad. "No I haven't."

"There are paper and pens over there. Write what you want and I'll get it fixed up in the buy and sell section."

"Thanks so much." She walked over and wrote the ad out as quick as she could. "One rabbit a few months old, free to good home." Then she added their phone number in the barn.

And then she turned around and handed the paper to him. He plucked it out of her hands and took it over to the reception desk. Then he turned around to face her again. "Jessica will take care of it for us."

She looked over at Jessica who was now staring at a computer screen.

Then she looked up. "Done."

"Thank you. How much is it?"

"Forget it. It won't be much, just a couple of dollars. I've got it covered. No arguments."

"Oh, thank you, Daniel. Then I insist on paying for lunch."

"No you don't. I won't have a lady paying for me."

Cherish couldn't help laughing at being called a lady. "Well, if you insist."

"I do." He took a step closer. "How far away is this coffee shop of yours?"

"Just a couple of blocks. It's not far at all."

Cherish couldn't have been happier when she sat down to eat with Daniel. She looked up at him and smiled, and her heart melted when he smiled back.

This was exactly the kind of man she could see

herself with. If only he was an Amish man. She was sure that he liked her too, otherwise why would he have suggested they go for coffee, and then expand it to lunch? Then again, she was the one who called him. He didn't call her, but maybe he would've. Perhaps he was just waiting until the news article about the orchard was published.

"So this is where you work, eh?" He stirred his cappuccino as she took a bite of her toasted cheese sandwich.

She quickly swallowed her mouthful. "I only do one shift a week now that Levi has got us all doing more around the orchard."

"And which do you prefer?"

"It's all the same to me. I have a farm you know."

His smile widened. "You do?"

"Yes. It was an inheritance. I can't wait to move there. It's kind of out in the middle of nowhere but that's just how I like it."

He shook his head. "I don't know how people can live anywhere that's isolated. I like the hustle and bustle of the big city. I've got my eyes set on New York City."

"You do?"

He nodded and then she knew he wasn't the right one for her. She liked the simple life on the farm, the life she used to have when she stayed with her dear aunt. Life on the farm wasn't always easy, but it was satisfying. Surely she couldn't have made a mistake about Daniel Withers. Up until now, he had seemed perfect. "Have you experienced life on a farm?"

"No."

Cherish laughed. "Then how do you know you wouldn't like it?"

"I like the buzz of having a crowd of people around, seeing people rushing to and from work. Sitting in a place like this. There are no busy cafés in the middle of nowhere."

With her spoon, Cherish carefully folded her chocolate sprinkles into the froth atop the coffee. "You should experience something before you say you don't like it."

"I guess that's true." He glanced at his watch. Right then Cherish knew he'd quickly decided that she wasn't for him.

"You in a hurry?" she asked.

"Not really. I do have to get back soon though. I've got to push this story through. The editor's looking it over again this afternoon. I think he's considering not running it. He said it wasn't exciting enough. I wouldn't be surprised if he made me rewrite it to give it more oomph."

"I thought it was just meant to be a simple story about plain folk."

"Me too, but they're always out to sell more papers. If I'm to be a good journalist I've got to find unique angles on things. Look behind what we see and hear— look for the truth."

"Oh." Cherish took a bite of her sandwich.

"I just want to be good at what I do. It's not about the money, it's about being good at something."

Cherish nodded and when she swallowed, she said, "I know what you mean."

"Do you?" That seemed to please him.

"I do."

"That ad will run in tomorrow's paper. That's right, isn't it?"

"That's so good. You don't want a rabbit, do you?"

"No. I can't have a pet. I've got to be ready to travel anywhere in the world. A pet would only slow me down."

"It sounds like you have an exciting life."

"It's not too exciting, but it could get that way at a moment's notice."

They smiled at each other, and once again, Cherish felt all was not lost. "Tell me about some of the stories you've done."

He grinned, and then proceeded to tell her about his career.

CHAPTER EIGHTEEN

*W*hen Cherish got home that afternoon, she witnessed a scene of great acting by Caroline. Cherish was quietly sitting at the kitchen table, having a cup of coffee with Wilma, when Caroline walked in crying followed by Favor.

"Something terrible has happened, Mrs. Bruner. I just called my folks to tell them I'm coming home and something dreadful has happened. First, when I switched my phone on I saw I had eleven missed calls from them."

"What is it?" Wilma asked.

"It's a terrible thing. It's my house. It's burned down."

Wilma stared at Caroline. "The whole house has gone?"

"That's right."

"Oh, that's terrible."

"It's the worst. Everything of mine is gone, my clothes, and … and everything."

"I'm so sorry to hear that, Caroline."

"My folks wanted me to ask you that, if it's all right with you, if I can stay a little while—at least until they get somewhere to live."

"Oh, where are they staying now?"

"They're living close by our house with a family friend, but there's no room for me. They only have a small house. And … we can't afford to live in a hotel."

"That's quite understandable. Not many people can. I'll talk to Mr. Bruner. I'm sure it will be okay to stay as long as you wish." Wilma stood. "Come here, you poor child."

Caroline stepped in and Wilma stood and wrapped her arms around her. When Wilma released her, she asked, "How did the fire start?"

"Electrical fault."

"Yes, I've heard that so often."

"At least you wouldn't have to worry about that here," Cherish said.

Everyone ignored her.

"Do you want me to call your parents and tell them you'll be fine with us for a while? I'm sure Mr. Bruner would like to speak with them as well. We'll assure them you'll be fine with us."

"No, it's not necessary. They've got so much going on. They trust you."

"Good thing their cell phones didn't go up in flames as well," Cherish said.

Caroline nodded. "That's right, or I wouldn't have been able to contact them."

"So, she can stay for sure?" asked Favor.

"As soon as *Dat* gets home, I'll ask him about it. I'm sure it will be fine."

"Thank you, Mrs. Bruner."

"What are you girls doing now?"

"Nothing."

"Caroline has something to ask you."

"What is it?"

"Mrs. Bruner, since I'll be here longer, will you show me how you make apple pies? I've never tasted anything like your apple pies."

Wilma put both hands to her face and laughed with delight. "I would love to show you. Who's in the shop?"

"Hope. They're having some of the rooms repainted at the bed and breakfast so she got to come home early. She's been helping us at the shop."

"Ah good. I have one hard-worker *dochder.*"

"I think *Mamm* means that you should both go back and help her."

"It doesn't need three," Favor said.

"It gets busy sometimes in the mid-afternoon."

"Cherish is right. Both of you go back and help Joy. Oh, I mean Hope. And, Caroline, I'll say it's okay for you to stay here. I don't want you worrying. I'm sure my husband wouldn't let you go home to a burned down house and have nowhere to stay."

"Thank you, Mrs. Bruner. I appreciate it."

THE NEXT DAY, when Cherish was having breakfast with her sisters and *Mamm*, they heard someone open the front door of the house and close it again.

"It must be *Dat* back from seeing what Isaac's done with the *haus*," Bliss said.

Before she'd even finished speaking, Ada burst into the kitchen with a newspaper clutched in her arms. "Read it, Wilma."

Wilma stood and took the paper. "What is it?"

"It's about the orchard and your whole family."

"Is it bad?" Bliss asked.

"It's horrifically horrible."

CHAPTER NINETEEN

*A*da slammed the newspaper down in front of Wilma. "Read it out loud so they can all hear," Ada said.

Wilma picked up the paper and held it in front of her. "A little way out of town, Bakers Apple Orchard can be found. It's owned by Amish man Levi Bruner, who took over the orchard when he married a widow. When you arrive, you will feel you have traveled back in time. If you're not tempted by the delightfully sweet apples you'll be tempted by the forbidden fruits that are Levi's stepdaughters."

Hope jumped up and ran to her mother. "This is dreadful."

Cherish grimaced. "Daniel can't have written that, did he?"

Caroline said, "You should complain, Mrs. Bruner. That's so awful."

"There's more," Ada said.

"Nee." *Mamm* shook her head. "I can't read any more."

When the phone in the barn rang, Cherish was the first out of the house to answer it. Breathlessly, she picked up the phone's receiver.

It was someone replying to her advertisement for the bunny. They wanted it for their eight-year-old. After asking some questions, Cherish was satisfied with them and gave them her address. They arranged to collect the rabbit at five that afternoon.

After she hung up the phone's receiver, she decided to call Daniel. She'd give him a chance to explain himself.

After he answered, she blurted out, "My whole family is upset over what you wrote."

"Cherish?"

"Yes, it's me."

"I'm mortified. I'm so sorry. I can explain. Hear me out. The story ran by accident. That wasn't the real story that I wrote. When I had some time yesterday I did another article about the orchard, for fun. It was just to make everyone in the office laugh. That's what we do. Most of us here write funny things that they wouldn't dare print. It's just for us, and we all do it."

"What happened then? How did it get printed instead of the real story?"

"I don't know. Someone's trying to sabotage me, that's all I can think."

Cherish blew out a deep breath. "My stepfather will be furious. Then there's the bishop. It just makes a mockery of us, all Amish people."

"I'm deeply sorry. I'll go there in person and apologize, explain what happened. I'm working up the nerve. I didn't think any of you Amish people would read the papers anyway."

"My mother's best friend saw it. She finds out everything."

Daniel sighed. "I'll give it a couple of days and come and see him, talk with him. I'll see if the paper will allow me to print some kind of an apology, or retraction."

"That would be good. In good news, I've got a taker for my rabbit."

"That is good news. I'm pleased for you."

"That'll make my mother happy, at least. I'll go tell her now."

"Cherish, do you think we could meet at your coffee shop tomorrow afternoon?"

Cherish was a little surprised. Maybe he really did like her. "Okay. What time?"

"Around two?"

"See you then." Cherish ended the call. She ran back to tell the others the good news about the rabbit.

When Levi arrived home hours later, everyone

ran out to meet him. He'd already seen the article in the paper and he'd already contacted the newspaper.

"What did they say?" asked Bliss, as her father got out of the buggy.

"They apologized and said they were going to print an apology."

They then looked down at the road as cars pulled up. "What's going on?" asked Levi.

"It's the shop," Wilma said. "We've never been so busy as we have this morning. We needed three girls there."

When five o'clock approached, Cherish asked Bliss to choose a rabbit. She reluctantly handed one over after kissing it and cuddling it goodbye. With the rabbit tucked under Cherish's arm, she made her way down to the shop to wait for the new owners. In the shop, she figured she'd be able to find a box for the rabbit. The new owners had said they were experienced with rabbits, so Cherish figured they'd already have food and a bed and everything at their home.

Just as she reached the door of the shop, a car pulled into the driveway. She'd spoken to a woman on the phone and there were two young men in the car. She held the rabbit firmly and approached the car.

"Are you one of the Baker girls?" one of the men called out.

"Yes. Have you come for the rabbit?"

"No. We've come to check out you Baker girls."

They both roared with laughter. Cherish knew it was because of the news report.

"Now you have seen me, so you can go away."

"Where are the others?"

Cherish frowned at them. "It's just me."

"What are you doing with Bugs Bunny?"

"He's going to a good home. You better get out of the driveway because the new owners are coming to pick him up any minute. The father is a policeman."

"Oooh, a scary policeman," one of them said.

The other said, "I think my dog would like a rabbit for dinner."

Cherish froze in fear when one of them opened the car door. "Your dog is not going anywhere near this rabbit. Goodbye." She held the rabbit firmly in her arms while she freed one hand to unlock the door of the shop.

When both men had gotten out of the car and were making sudden movements in her direction, the rabbit jumped out of her arms. The key fell to the ground as Cherish made a lunge for the rabbit. She missed. Then the rabbit hopped away around the corner. "Get out of here," Cherish screamed at the men, but they just laughed and one of them chased the rabbit.

Cherish opened her mouth and screamed as loud as she could. It'd worked for her when she was younger and she hoped it would bring people running.

The man who stayed near the car was shocked and

said, "Steady on. We're going." He opened the door and got back in.

Cherish opened her mouth and screamed again.

The man in the car called to his friend, "Let's get out of here. She's crazy."

"I nearly got it," the man yelled back.

Cherish couldn't let that happen. She picked up a broom that was leaning against the shop and went after the man who was running after the rabbit. While she was doing that, the car was reversed down the driveway. It seemed he was going to leave his friend there.

Then she noticed Levi not far ahead of them. He was running at them.

When the rabbit saw Levi dashing at him, he darted off into the direction of the orchard. When the young man saw Levi, he turned away and ran back to the car which was now on the road facing the other direction. The man jumped in the car and it sped away.

"Are you okay, Cherish?" Levi asked when he reached her.

She was out of breath. "I'm fine. They were here because of the news report. They wanted to see the Baker girls, they said. I thought they were the ones coming to get the rabbit. They'll be coming to pick up the rabbit at any time now and now it has escaped."

"That's not good. Wilma will be furious that he's gotten into the orchard. Let's go."

"We have to get him."

Both Levi and Cherish ran after the rabbit who now

appeared as a white dot in the distance. Cherish knew in her heart it was useless, but still, she had to try for Bliss's sake.

Levi slowed down. "You keep your eyes on him. I'll go back and get Bliss. We'll need food or something to entice him."

"Okay. I'll try."

"You must do it, Cherish. Bliss will be so upset if he's lost in the wilderness."

"I'll do it."

Once the rabbit got under the cover of some bushes, he slowed down. Cherish didn't want to spook him again, so she kept her distance and let him calm down.

Before long, Bliss came with the mother rabbit.

That did the trick. Bliss sat a distance from the baby rabbit and it hopped over to Bliss and its mother.

Cherish tucked the broom she was still carrying under her arm and carried the mother back to the house while Bliss held the baby.

Then Levi called out to them that the people were here to take the rabbit.

Bliss said to Cherish, "I'm going to give them another one. Not this one. He's had too much excitement for one day."

"*Jah,* good idea," said Cherish. "I'm so sorry, Bliss. We nearly lost him."

"It's not your fault. It was the fault of those horrible men. *Dat* told me about it."

In that moment, Cherish realized that Bliss was so

distracted by what had happened that she didn't seem that sad to be giving away the rabbit.

"I just hope the people are nice," Bliss said squinting at the house as they walked back to it.

"I talked to the woman on the phone and she was lovely."

"Good. I've prayed that they'll all go to nice people."

As Cherish walked, she realized she was still holding onto the broom. She went back to put it in the shop and found the key on the ground. A shiver traveled down her spine thinking about those horrible men.

CHAPTER TWENTY

*I*t had been days since Cherish had brought their father's will to Florence.

It certainly looked like an official will, and had her father's signature on it. Even Carter thought it was legitimate.

After Florence put her sleeping baby down in the crib, she wandered over to the photocopy machine where Carter had left the copied will. Florence picked it up and stared at her father's signature. It was the same as she'd seen hundreds of times before when she'd helped him with the bookwork and been by his side when he'd signed the checks.

She ran her fingertips lightly over the curves of the B in Baker.

Her stomach lurched. She missed her father so. If only she had one more minute with him. If she was granted one more minute, she'd spend it walking through the orchard with him. No words would need be spoken. It would be enough that he was there by her side. Tears fell down her cheeks.

He'd been the only person who really understood her, really knew her.

Carter coming into her life had been a blessing, but nothing replaced her father or removed the pain his death had caused. Her heart was fractured and Wilma hiding the will was like pouring iodine into an open wound. Wilma's iodine wasn't the healing kind. It was the festering kind that had nothing healing about it.

Florence put the will back down, reminding herself that it wouldn't happen unless it was God who had His hand on her getting the orchard back. He was in control and not Wilma.

She grabbed hold of the photocopied will again and headed downstairs and into the kitchen which, for the moment, doubled as Carter's office until the new home was built.

He looked up. "What's that you have there?"

She turned around to face him. "It's my father's will."

"I thought it might be." He closed the lid of his laptop. "So, what are your thoughts?"

"I feel I have to say something, do something. At least let Wilma know that I know about it. Things are more complicated now that Wilma is married and there is a new head of the family. I guess Levi's trying to do his best to run the orchard and provide for them. And what annoys me is that not long ago he was talking about selling and then as soon as we want to buy it, he recoils from that idea."

Carter slowly nodded, and Florence knew he was trying to be supportive even though he wanted her to drop any thoughts of doing anything at all about the will.

"When *Dat* died, it wasn't long before Levi started coming around. I knew he didn't like me and I wasn't overly fond of him. The man was dull, never had anything to say and he ignored me most of the time. He swooped in on Wilma as soon as I left to marry you. It was as though he was lying in wait to get Wilma in her time of weakness and trap her into marrying him."

Carter laughed. "You have such a way of putting things."

"That's how I see it."

She leaned against the countertop. "Will you talk to a lawyer?"

"Yes. If that's what you want, but it might be best if you and Wilma talk about it first. It's best if we can come to some friendly conclusion."

Florence sighed. "You're right. It'll be unpleasant, though."

"Will that get Cherish into trouble?" he asked.

"I don't think I have to mention her. Now that I know *Dat* told Earl and Mark about it, I could simply say I am aware that there is a will, and I'll tell her that I know what it says in the will. Then I'll see what she says from there."

"Playing it by ear then, eh?"

"I guess so. I know they're not going to just hand the orchard over."

"No, I can't see them doing that."

"Especially since Wilma covered up everything. Anyway, I'll make us some coffee before I think about what we'll have for dinner. I'll have to think through what I'll say to Wilma. I won't go there today or tomorrow. I'll go the day after. You don't have any appointments, do you? I don't want to take Iris with me."

"I'll make sure I'm home all day."

"Thank you." With a flick of a switch, Florence turned on the coffee machine. "Perhaps I should talk to someone who can give me another opinion."

"Like who?"

"Christina."

CHAPTER TWENTY-ONE

*C*hristina opened her door, and smiled at Florence.

"Come in."

Florence walked past her. "I have some news and I don't know how you'll take it."

"Let's sit on the couch." Once they were seated, Christina said, "You're having another baby. Congratulations. I knew that would happen. I'm happy for you."

Florence frowned. Her sister-in-law wasn't letting her get a word out. "Christina."

"It's perfectly fine Florence, I'm happy for you."

"No, it's not that."

"Wait. Wilma's not having a *boppli,* is she?"

Florence shook her head. "No, but I have something to tell you about Wilma."

"What's she done now?"

"Cherish surprised me and Carter the other day. You'll never guess what she brought over."

"A stray cat. No wait, a bunny. No, that would've been Bliss. What did Cherish do?"

"She brought my father's will."

"Hasn't that all been settled? It's been years now."

"That's just it. No one ever knew that he had one. Everything was just transferred to Wilma."

"Did the will say any different?"

"Well, I hope you won't be upset by this, but the orchard wasn't left to Mark."

"That wouldn't matter to me or Mark. He's never been interested in the orchard and neither was Earl. Wait, who was it left to?"

"To me. His wishes were that Wilma and everyone in the family had a home to live there for the rest of their lives, if they wanted, but the orchard was to be mine."

"That would be a bit awkward. Not about you owning the orchard but people living there if you didn't want them to. Now that things aren't so good between you and Wilma. Wait a minute, what happens now, then?"

"That's the odd thing. That will was hidden away and no one knows Cherish found it."

"Oh, so Wilma was hiding it and Cherish has found it. So Wilma doesn't know that you know."

"That's right. The thing is Wilma was named as

executor and it appears that she's just hid the will away in her room."

"What are you going to do?"

Florence sighed. "I don't know."

"You could've brought Iris with you."

Florence smiled. "She was sleeping. I'll bring her next time."

"Good. Never come here alone."

"I won't. Carter says they're not going to hand the orchard over. It's all complicated now because Wilma is married to Levi, and what's going to happen there? Where will they live? Carter thinks I should leave things well and truly alone. He says he'll help me and support me, but I know that is what he's thinking."

"Still, it will cause a lot of complications."

"What am I to do? Do you know how I feel about the orchard?"

"You have your own now."

"Yes, but it's not my father's."

"No it's not. It's yours and Carters. When you really get down to it, it's just a piece of land, isn't it, with a few trees—bark and leaves? What's really important, Florence, is that you have everything. And if you're here complaining to me that you don't have the orchard, or that you want the orchard or anything like that, I don't have any sympathy for you at all."

"Why not?"

"I would give everything I own and then some to have a little one like Iris. That's what's really important.

SAMANTHA PRICE

And look at your husband, he's devoted to you. You have everything you ever wanted. A comfortable home, no wait that's not good enough for you, you're building a brand-new home and you also bought the Jenkin's orchard. You now have two orchards, a baby, and Carter's building you a huge home. Look what you have, Florence. You have it all already. Why be greedy?"

Florence considered what her sister-in-law said. "You're right, I do feel kind of silly. I knew you'd make me see sense. I just had to talk it over with someone. You don't mind do you?"

"No. I'm glad you felt you could come to me. I've cried on your shoulder enough times. I don't mind being there for you."

"Thank you, Christina. You really are my only friend now. I find it quite hard to meet people. Very few Amish folk want anything to do with me now, but you've always been a good friend to me since I left the Amish."

"You're my husband's sister. And we both haven't had an easy road in life."

The orchard was nothing in the scheme of things. She had her memories.

But it still nagged at her why Wilma thought she could keep quiet about the will for all these years.

It just wasn't right.

"I'll make us a pot of tea," Christina said.

"I'll help."

CHAPTER TWENTY-TWO

The next day, Cherish sat with the reporter, Daniel Withers, at the coffee shop.

She told him how those two men had come to the Bakers' place after reading the news article, how they'd harassed her, startled the poor little bunny right out of her arms, and then had chased the rabbit away.

"I'm so sorry. I'm an idiot."

"It's not your fault."

He sighed and looked into his coffee. "I've made a mess of things. Here I was thinking I'm going to be some big-time reporter. I was going to go from the paper to the TV and end up an anchorman. They say I've got a good voice for it, and a good face."

"All's not lost, and you do have a nice face, handsome even."

He glanced up at her and smiled, but that smile didn't last long. "I think I'm done for."

"Just go to your bosses and apologize, and go to my stepfather."

"The bosses know what happened, but they're still blaming me. No use apologizing to them. They know the score. Someone sabotaged me and I don't know who it was. I'll probably never find out. I'll just have to watch my back. I will apologize to Mr. Bruner properly and in person, but not just yet. I need a break from the stress."

"What did you say to your bosses about what you did?"

"I was trying to make the orchard sound exciting. I mean, it's just a bunch of apple trees. You grow them, pick them, eat them. I was trying to cause a sensation, make my colleagues laugh. Like I told you on the phone yesterday, they know it wasn't my real story. They don't care."

"Well, you caused a sensation. Our little shop's never been busier than this morning and yesterday." Cherish giggled.

"That might make your stepfather happy."

"He does like money, but it's my mother who's unhappiest."

"I'm sorry." He sighed again. "I've never done so much apologizing in my life."

"I know what you mean. I upset people all the time. I've given up saying I'm sorry now unless I'm forced to do it."

Daniel looked up from his coffee and smiled. "What could you possibly have done that's so bad?"

"Nothing much. Nothing much lately. It's just that I'm older in the head than my family thinks I am. I've been an adult for years, but my years don't tell the truth of my maturity. My years say I'm still a kid, not yet an adult. I've got a grown-up mind."

"That's how I felt when I was growing up. Thanks for meeting me here today. I needed to … talk to someone. It's helping me feel better. I hope I haven't ruined my life and possibly that of your family."

"No. I'm sure you're not the only reporter who's tried to make a bigger story out of something."

He laughed. "Yes, but they wouldn't have so many people upset with them and nearly lose their jobs over it."

"Are you sure?"

"Yes. Well maybe not, but my newspaper is more conservative than most."

"Why don't you work for a less conservative one?"

He nodded. "That's a very good question, one I've been giving a lot of thought to. You see the problem is that I need to work for a respectable newspaper if I want to end up where I'm aiming. I can't do it going down the other route."

"Pick yourself up, dust yourself off and apologize to everyone. The sooner you do that, the sooner you can go back to work and all will be forgotten." Cherish knew it would be a long time before her mother and Ada forgot it, but that wouldn't affect Daniel.

"I know you're right." He sighed again. When his face lit up, Cherish looked around to see what he was grinning at.

It was Caroline. She'd just walked into the café with Favor. *"Ach,* what are they doing here?"

"I recognize Caroline from her social media. That's how I found the video about your community."

"The other one is my sister. Caroline's her pen pal. She's staying with us for a while."

"I heard that somewhere. Possibly from your stepfather."

Cherish frowned at him. He hadn't taken his eyes off Caroline since she'd walked in. When Favor and Caroline finished placing their order at the counter, they walked toward them.

"It's okay if you have to leave now." Cherish spoke quickly to Daniel before they got there. She could already see what was going to happen. The writing was on the wall.

He shook his head, and he wasn't even looking at Cherish when he said, "No, I need another cup of coffee." His eyes were still on Caroline.

Cherish couldn't blame him. Caroline was very attractive. "Daniel, order one at the counter and tell them I'll pay for it."

He looked at her this time. "No, I'll pay for it, Cherish. What would you like?"

"I'm fine, thanks."

He got up to order another cup of coffee just before the two girls sat down.

"Who's that?" Caroline asked when she sat down. "Is that the reporter? I've met him before, I'm sure."

"Jah, the reporter that *Mamm* is mad at. He's going to say he's sorry. He's coming to the house soon to speak with Levi. Not today, but soon."

"That's good."

"Why are you talking to him?" Favor asked.

"I know him. He talked to me at the house before he ever talked to Levi. What are you two doing in here? Have you been following me?"

"No. You're not that important, Cherish," Caroline told her. "You have the biggest ego, bigger than anyone I know and I know many people."

Favor giggled until Cherish scowled at her.

"Did I invite either of you to sit with us on our date?" Cherish asked.

"Nee, but he left. You mean, he's coming back?" Favor asked.

"Jah, he's just gone to get another cup of coffee."

Favor and Caroline exchanged smiles, and that was when Cherish knew they were up to no good. Had they overheard her this morning when she told Hope she was meeting the reporter at the café? Most likely.

Daniel sat back down with them and Cherish introduced them.

"I already know you, Caroline. It was because of you

I thought of doing a story about the apple orchard. That video you uploaded to the internet got so many hits. I traced it back to you."

"Is that right?" She smiled at him.

"It is." He leaned forward slightly. "So, Caroline, you're visiting the Baker family?"

"That's right. Favor and I have been pen pals for years now. We were always saying we were going to visit one another and finally, I did."

"I have a confession to make. I've been following you on social media for a while. Particularly your YouTube channel. When I saw the video about the Amish gathering I took it to my editor. I thought there was a story there."

"Yes, there are lots of stories surrounding my family," said Cherish thinking of one story in particular—about a hidden will.

"Well, I was blamed for doing that and I had to take it down. I'm glad you got to see it at least." Caroline flashed a bright smile at him, revealing her perfectly even and whiter-than-white teeth.

He gave a smile back, equally as wide which annoyed Cherish even further.

"Seems the Amish like to keep their secrets," Daniel said.

"Yes, And there are other things I could tell you about the Baker family. Wilma, in particular."

"But you won't, will you?" Favor asked Caroline, frowning at her.

Cherish held her breath. Favor would've been silly enough to tell Caroline everything about their family.

"No, because it's a story you see all the time about children who've been born out of wedlock meeting up again with the real mothers when the children have grown."

He leaned closer, his face now serious. "Tell me more."

Cherish put her hands up, breaking their locked gaze. "It's not a story that needs to be told."

"An Amish woman having a child out of wedlock, is that what you're saying? Wilma? Isn't that your mother, Cherish, and yours, Favor? Or are you talking about one of the Baker girls? No. It can't be one of you Baker girls because the child would not be old enough yet to meet up with one of you."

Favor and Cherish stared at each other not knowing what to say.

"It must happen all the time," Caroline said. "It's not interesting to me, but it must be interesting to some because there are programs about it on TV. My mom watches them and cries."

"Yes, it could be interesting," Daniel said, "depending on how it's told."

Favor shook her head. "It could happen all the time, but, if it happens all the time, it happens in secret because it is supposed to be a secret. Because it's no one else's business, and it just doesn't involve one person."

The waitress brought over three coffees and placed them down on the table. "You're not having a second, Cherish?"

"No. Not today."

When the waitress left, Daniel said, "There's no need to worry. As much as that sounds like an intriguing story, that's not the kind of reporter I'm aiming to be. I don't want to do scandals and intrigue, or even feel-good warm and fuzzies. I want to do proper stories, important ones."

"I've always wanted to be a journalist," said Caroline.

"You have?" Daniel asked, his smile returning.

She nodded enthusiastically. "That's what I'm studying to be."

Cherish stared at her. She wasn't so sure that was true; she'd said she was only going to college to get her parents off her back.

"Perhaps I could help in some way?" he said.

"That would be wonderful."

"We could get together some time and I can tell you what it's like."

"I'd really like that. I'll give you my phone number. Give me your cell phone?" Caroline held out her hand toward Daniel.

He reached into his pocket, pulled it out, and handed it over. She punched in her name and the numbers and handed it back to him.

Cherish marveled at how easy that was. If only she had a cell phone too.

"I'll send you a text." He tapped on his phone. "There. Now you have my number. Call me any time."

Favor was quick to point out, "She won't be able to use it in our house though, she can only use it outside the house."

Caroline got her phone out of her bag and looked at it. "That's right. I turn it off as soon as I enter the house." She tapped her screen several times, saving his information.

"I understand. I'll send you a message and then you can give me a call back. Perhaps I will arrange something in the next couple of days."

Caroline nodded. "I'd really like that."

"How long are you staying with the Bakers?"

"We're not too sure," said Cherish answering for Caroline before she got a chance. "At first it was only going to be a day, and then it got extended … and then extended again." Cherish had nearly given up. How could she compete for Daniel's attention while wearing shapeless dresses, aprons, and a cap that covered her beautiful long hair? She might be just as beautiful as Caroline if she too could wear make-up and suitable clothes that showed she had a figure.

Daniel must've found her and her sisters pretty to make that remark in the papers, but it was clear Caroline had caught his attention. Just when she was contemplating whether she should forget him or not, she thought of something. "Caroline will be here at least until her home is rebuilt after the tragedy."

Daniel looked at Caroline. "What happened?"

"Nothing."

"Her home was burnt down." Cherish looked over at Caroline. "I heard you telling Levi."

Caroline picked up a spoon and stirred the froth in her cappuccino with her head hung. "Oh, that. I'll tell you about that later, Daniel."

"That might be something I could write about. It sounds intriguing."

"It's really not." Caroline picked up her cup and sipped her coffee.

Favor said, "We have to go soon, Caroline. *Mamm's* showing you how to make apple pies this afternoon."

Caroline rolled her eyes. "That's if she doesn't find something more important to do. She was supposed to help me make pies the other day and she didn't."

"I love apple pies," said Daniel.

Caroline looked over and smiled at him. "I'll bake one especially for you."

"Would you?"

Cherish knew it was no use. She couldn't compete. "I should get back to relieve our mother. She's helping Hope in the shop until I get back."

CHAPTER TWENTY-THREE

*A*fter a late afternoon session of apple pie making, the girls were busy cleaning up from that and helping Wilma prepare dinner when Levi walked into the kitchen. "I've just come back from meeting with the bishop about this newspaper thing."

They all looked up at him to hear what Bishop Paul had said. Levi had been called to his house to discuss the article in the newspaper.

"The suggestion was that I'm to ask Mr. Withers to do a positive news story. How do I set about doing that?" he asked the girls.

"Call him and ask him," Cherish said.

"*Jah*, do it, *Dat*," Bliss said.

"He gave you his card with his phone number on it," Cherish reminded him.

"*Jah* and I still have that somewhere. I'll call him and ask him. There's no harm in that."

"What kind of a story would he do?" asked Bliss.

"I don't know."

Cherish thought of a story … maybe even two. A story where a wicked woman hid her husband's will from everyone, but that wouldn't be a positive story. Neither would a story about a young woman who pretended her house burned down so she could prolong her stay in the Amish community.

"Levi, I talked to Daniel today. So did Caroline and Favor."

He took off his hat. "I'm listening."

"I can talk to him again, if you'd like. I'll ask him to come to the *haus* so you can speak with each other and say what you want."

"*Denke,* Cherish. That sounds like a mighty fine idea."

Mamm rose from her chair. "Sit down in the living room, Levi. I'll make you a cup of hot tea."

Levi smiled at Wilma, turned and walked out of the room.

Cherish wasted no time getting to the phone in the barn before Caroline called Daniel from her cell phone. It had weighed on her mind all the way back home that she had to speak with him.

She grabbed the phone and entered his number. "Hello Daniel, it's me, Cherish Baker."

"Hi, Cherish. I was just thinking about you and your sisters and your lovely guest."

Cherish scoffed. "Not so lovely. I called to ask you

not to run that story Caroline told you about—the illegitimate child, the one born out of wedlock. It's a very personal thing to my family and it would embarrass my mother so much if that got out."

"Tell me about it."

"I can't. I suppose I could if you promise you wouldn't run the story."

"I told you I don't want to be that kind of reporter, but I am intrigued."

"There's not a lot to it. My mother had a child out of wedlock and that's not unusual. I've heard of that happening before, and I don't think she's bad, she's not a bad person—she's a bit irritating sometimes, but she's not a bad person."

"I know, I didn't say that she was."

Cherish licked her lips. "It was when she was young before she got married to my father, her first husband. She had the child and then gave him to her sister to raise and then she didn't have any more to do with him or her sister. Then when the child grew up, he was curious about his roots and he bought a house next door to my mother when both his parents had died."

"Adoptive parents you mean?"

"Here's where it gets a bit confusing. His adoptive mother was his aunt, but the man his aunt ended up marrying was the boy's biological father because they got to know each other through her looking after his child, you see? He had visitation rights to the child and the two of them fell in love."

"I'm following so far; that makes sense. So this man, I assume he's a man now, he'd be your half-brother?"

"Yeah."

"He moved next door and then what happened?"

"Nothing. He didn't tell anybody who he was or anything. He just wanted to live there and observe the family I guess. He never had any intention of telling anyone about it at all. Then my half-sister from my father's first marriage fell in love with him. They got married and now they have a child. A baby girl. She's adorable and she's my niece."

"I see. It's like a soap opera. Many threads, marriages, births ... and all these threads tie your family together with a large bow. Or you could say, these many threads make an Amish quilt." He chuckled.

"Oh, I like that. You do have a way with words."

"I hope so. That's what I'm paid for."

"I guess so, but the thing is it would really hurt my mother and everybody else if this got out. So please, don't say a word. It could destroy lives, and sadden people. I don't know what would happen. And Levi, who had no part in any of this would be embarrassed and probably want to move away."

"Doesn't he know?"

"He would know, but he wouldn't want to talk about it. Or *read* about it."

"Interesting."

"Good, so you won't?" asked Cherish, holding her breath. For some reason, she trusted him.

"I didn't say that."

Cherish heard him laughing and gasped a deep breath. She was unable to speak, which was unusual for her.

"I'm teasing you, Cherish."

"Don't do that." She put her hand on her chest. "My heart nearly stopped beating."

"You've got an interesting life, Cherish Baker."

"Do you really think so?"

"In comparison, mine's boring even with the official caution the newspaper's given me. Why don't you call me next time you're coming into town? I'd love to catch up with you again."

Cherish couldn't believe her ears. Did he like her and not Caroline? Or did he like both of them? "I'll do that. Oh, and stop by the house soon, would you? My stepfather would like you to come here and that would be the perfect time for you to apologize. He wants to ask you if you can do a positive story."

"I'll come as soon as I can. How does tomorrow sound? I can be there around fiveish."

"Around five? Perfect. I'll let Levi know. Bye." She ended the call, having forgotten to wait for him to say goodbye.

CHAPTER TWENTY-FOUR

*L*ater that night, it was raining heavily and the girls couldn't go outside to talk after dinner, so the Baker girls and Caroline huddled together in Favor's bedroom.

Caroline sat on the windowsill smoking with the window up slightly, trying to direct the smoke outside.

"Who do you like, Cherish?" Favor asked her.

"I like Daniel, the reporter."

"So do I. Too bad," said Caroline.

Cherish scowled. "Too bad for you. I spotted him first when he came to do the story."

"Oh, Cherish, not this again," Hope said. You did the same thing with Bliss. Just because you saw Adam Wengerd first you think you can make him love you, but you can't. Not everyone's going to love you. You get enough male attention."

159

"Yeah, Cherish, leave some men for the rest of us," Favor said, causing Caroline and Bliss to giggle.

Cherish jumped to her feet, annoyed, and said to Caroline. "Favor hates it that you kicked her out of her bed."

When everyone was shocked to silence at her outburst, Cherish turned and walked out the door and closed it behind her. Then she listened at the door.

"Favor, did you say that to Cherish?" she heard Caroline ask.

"Um, I said something about you being *in* the bed."

"If you're upset, then why not talk to me about it? We're taking turns in the bed now anyway." Caroline pouted.

"It's okay. There's no problem."

Cherish kept listening.

Caroline said, "If my parents knew I was sleeping on the floor, though, they'd be so upset."

"It's fine. I don't mind sleeping there. The floor's not even that hard."

Cherish put her hand over her mouth and giggled about Favor saying the floor wasn't hard. It was a wooden floor. Of course it was hard.

Upset over Daniel liking Caroline and Caroline not objecting to his attention, Cherish walked downstairs for some company. There had been a glimmer of hope, but then that glimmer got duller when she remembered how Daniel did not take his eyes from Caroline.

No one was in the kitchen or the living room. A

single gas lamp burned in the kitchen giving off a soft glow. She slung a shawl over her shoulders and stepped from the back of the house into the cool night air. The rain had stopped and the air smelled fresh.

She looked at the step where she wanted to sit and saw it was still wet. She took off her shawl, folded it over and sat down on it . Soon she was joined by her dog. "Hi, Caramel. Sit down and be still. I need to think for a moment."

An owl hooted and Cherish looked up to see if she could spot it. It was somewhere within the darkness behind the barn. Most likely in one of the trees. It reminded her of years ago when *Dat* tried to attract barn owls to keep down the rodents. He'd put boxes in the trees. She'd forgotten about that until now. No one had taken those boxes down, she was sure of that. Maybe the owl had found one of them. That memory made her feel good inside, reminding her of happier, simpler days when her family was nicer to her and she wasn't in trouble every five minutes.

Everything had changed when *Dat* died and then things got so much worse when Florence left suddenly.

Cherish sighed and looked at Caramel. "If I were a dog, my life would be so much less complicated. I could run in the fields, roll around in the dirt, and I wouldn't have to be bothered by these stupid clothes with yards of useless fabric. If I had a choice, I'd wear something much more simple."

The owl hooted once more.

"I'd like to be free as a bird, having flown the nest. I'd go wherever I pleased and would never be troubled by anything." She rested her head on top of Caramel's and was comforted by his warmth. "I can't wait until we get to the farm. There won't be another living soul for miles, except for Ruth next door. There'll be no one who'll bother us and no one for me to worry about offending. We'll go to one meeting a month. I don't see that it'll be necessary to do the second meeting thing every month. The households of the community members are spread too many miles apart."

She hugged Caramel, the only being who truly understood her, and he gave her a lick on the face before she could stop him. Giggling, she wiped her face.

"You're truly my only friend. People are weird. You never let me down." Behind her she heard the door open.

"What are you doing out here in the dark?" *Mamm* asked.

"I'm listening to an owl."

"Good. Owls are our friends."

Cherish twisted further to face her mother. "Why are you still awake?"

"I'm worried about this thing in the newspaper. At the start, I told the reporter to go away, do you remember?"

"I do. You said Levi wouldn't want to talk with him, but Levi did."

"Jah, and look what a fine mess we're in now. And I'm also worried about Caroline's parents having no place to live. Such a dreadful thing to lose a house and every single thing you own."

"I wouldn't worry about them. I'm sure they'll be fine."

"Do you think so?"

"Jah. Caroline was only making it sound worse so she could stay longer. I'm sure of that. It's just a feeling I have, but I'm usually right."

"If that's true then I'm pleased. I don't mind her staying longer. She's a delightful girl and she fits in here well. She's no trouble."

"Not to you maybe," Cherish said under her breath.

Wilma took another step toward her. "What?"

"Nothing. And it'll all work out with that reporter too. He's nice. I've talked to him a few times. He helped me put the ad in the paper for the rabbit."

"Did he? He's nice if he helps people. I only met him the once."

"He explained what happened. He said it was a joke. It wasn't supposed to be published. That wasn't the real story that was supposed to be in the paper."

"It was still printed though. Mistake or no mistake. It was horrible."

"Sometimes nice people can do horrible things though, don't you think?" Cherish asked, thinking about the will.

"If they do, they admit it and apologize and set things right."

"Oh, they set things right?"

"*Jah*, they do."

"And, if the thing they've done has changed the course of someone's life, a good person will do everything they can to set things right?"

"*Jah*. I believe so."

"Interesting." At that moment, the owl hooted again.

"I hear it now. Well, I should go back to bed. I was just going to make myself a hot cup of tea. Do you want one?"

"*Nee, denke*. I'll sit here for a little longer and enjoy the quiet."

"If that's what you want."

"It is."

"Aren't you cold? It's freezing out here."

"I'm fine. Caramel's keeping me warm."

"*Gut nacht,* Cherish."

"Night, *Mamm.*"

CHAPTER TWENTY-FIVE

*T*he next day, Cherish was excited because Daniel was coming to talk with Levi. Every time she heard a car, she'd look out the window of the shop where she was working, hoping it was him. Now it was getting late and he still hadn't shown.

Favor was working with her today and they had been run off their feet, to the point *Mamm* had to leave off making preserves and dried fruit to help them. Caroline was supposed to be there today, helping in the shop, and she wasn't.

Favor had avoided Cherish's questions about Caroline's whereabouts, and Cherish figured Caroline had snuck off to see Daniel. Then, when she saw Daniel's car turn into the driveway with Caroline in the front seat, she was furious.

There was nothing she could do because she had two customers, and Favor had walked out the door to meet her friend. Then, instead of Caroline bypassing the shop and heading to the house with Daniel like Cherish thought she would, she walked into the shop with Favor and pulled an apron from the wall, tying it up behind her back.

Cherish knew immediately what she was up to. Caroline was going to pretend she'd been there all day.

Caroline was ruthless.

Cherish held her tongue until the customers left. Then she said, "What were you doing out with Daniel? You know I like him, I told you I did."

"Yes, and I told you I did too. He asked me out, he didn't ask you."

"I was talking to him last night and he asked me out again. *Jah,* I said, 'again.'"

Caroline shrugged her shoulders. "If you say so."

"It's because you're always flirting, batting your eyelashes at him and wearing tight clothes. That's something I can't do."

"That's not my fault. Besides, you can if you want. You can leave your community. Do it if you want."

"I'm too young or I wouldn't be here still."

"If you're too young to leave the community, you're too young for a man like Daniel. Sorry. Now, what am I supposed to do when there are no customers? It's a waste of time me being here. I'll just go up to the house."

"You're supposed to polish the apples." She handed her a cloth.

"'Polish' them? I've never heard of such a thing."

"Yes. Polish them, to make them bright and shiny. It makes them more appealing."

"They already look appealing enough, Cherish, and I don't think there'll be any more customers today. Can't we close up?"

"Nee. We will wait until five. You asked me what to do, Caroline, and I told you. If you don't want to do that just go back to the house. But I'll not cover for you. I'm not going to lie to my family and say you were here all day. *Mamm* knows you weren't here most of the day anyway. She had to help when we got busy."

Caroline put her hands on her hips. "I'll make an excuse to her. You shouldn't have told Daniel that my house burned down. How could you be so mean?"

"I was just repeating it. It's not my lie, it's yours. Favor told me to say it."

"Is that right?"

Favor's mouth fell open as both girls looked at her. "I did not!"

"I believe you," Caroline told her. "Keep your beak out of my life, Cherish Baker." She took the apron off, rolled it up and threw it at Cherish, and then turned on her heel and walked out of the shop.

Cherish picked up the apron and threw it back, but it just landed in the doorway since Caroline had left. Cherish couldn't wait until Caroline went home. Their guest was such a big liar, and Cherish wanted to be around when Levi and her mother found out the truth.

Maybe Caroline was only staying around because of Daniel. She'd thought it was for Adam or Fairfax, but she could've been wrong. Or, did Caroline like all three men?

When Favor walked out without a word, Cherish was still furious. They'd left the closing-up job for her. Neither of them had done a proper day's work. Favor was too slow serving the customers and had trouble counting out the change.

How in the world had Florence done what she'd done after *Dat* died? She ran the farm, made all the decisions, ran the household and opened the shop in the warmer months of the year. All that with next to no help from Wilma. Cherish felt awful that she hadn't helped Florence more.

Cherish looked in the cash drawer. They'd made a tidy sum today.

Levi would be pleased.

She emptied the takings into a bag and then started on the nightly closing procedures, which involved sweeping and dusting, and making sure they had enough bags, boxes, and stock for the next day.

When she headed back to the house, Daniel was just leaving. He looked up at her and waved. She hurried over to him with the money bag firmly in her hand.

"Daniel, I was hoping to speak with you before you talked to Levi. I got delayed."

"It's all good. I apologized and he accepted my apology."

"Oh. What else was said?"

Daniel looked back at the house and waved to Levi and Wilma who were standing there waiting for him to get in the car. They waved back and, when they saw that he wasn't going right away, they turned and went back inside. "You were right. He wants me to do another story about the orchard. A good news story, but really, I don't think I can. It's not up to me. I explained that to Mr. Bruner. I think he understood."

"There are no stories here—none."

He smiled at her. "None that I'm prepared to write about."

"Thanks." She smiled back.

He walked to his car. "Don't forget to call me."

She glanced back at the house and wondered where Caroline was. Why wasn't she out here saying goodbye to him? "Bye, I will call."

When she went back into the house, she found Caroline in the kitchen peeling vegetables for dinner.

"Daniel just left," Cherish announced to everyone.

"Jah, he came in and said goodbye to us."

Caroline didn't even look up at her. When Caroline had first arrived, Cherish wanted to be her friend, but now the young woman was getting in her way.

"Are you going to stand there, or help, Cherish?" *Mamm* asked.

"I'll give this money to Levi and then I'll wash my hands."

"Ada's coming for dinner and we're running late."

Cherish wasn't sure how she felt about Ada coming. That woman always had something to say about everything.

CHAPTER TWENTY-SIX

*C*herish had been right about Ada having a lot to say. In the middle of dinner, she said, "What we need is a family dinner to brighten everyone up."

"Good idea. Christina and Mark haven't been here for ages," Hope said.

Wilma pursed her lips, Cherish knew she didn't think of her stepson and his wife as family—not anymore. The couple staying away from all the family events didn't help things at all. Christina didn't even come to help at harvest time like she had in previous years when Florence had been in charge.

Ada didn't stop there. "Bliss, you can invite Adam and Hope can invite Fairfax."

"*Denke.* He'd like that I'm sure," said Bliss.

Ada turned to Wilma. "Your birthday is coming up. We should make the dinner your birthday dinner."

"*Nee.* We don't have to do that. We can still have a dinner. It doesn't have to be for my birthday."

"I think we should do it. We haven't seen Mark in ages." Cherish reinforced what Hope had said about their half brother. "We can invite everyone."

Ada said, "I will invite Christina myself. If she agrees to come, Mark will come with her."

After a while, *Mamm* spoke. "We could invite her, but I don't think Mark would come."

"At least we could invite them," Favor said. "I miss Mark, and Earl too."

"*Jah,* we should. He is part of this family," Bliss said.

"Exactly." Cherish looked down and glanced up at Ada from under her lashes. She wondered what Ada would think about what *Mamm* had done with the will.

Unless Ada was the one who had encouraged Wilma to keep quiet about it.

Nee. Ada was too good and righteous to be involved in something like that. Her mother, on the other hand…

"I could make a big German cherry cake with dark chocolate grated on the top just the way you like it," Ada said.

"I do like a German cherry cake," *Mamm's* mouth curled upward at the corners.

"Just name all of your favorite food and the girls and I will cook it all."

Mamm shrugged her shoulders and her smile disappeared. "I don't know. It's all such a fuss."

Bliss said, "Won't you allow us to do something for you, *Mamm?*"

Wilma smiled fondly at her stepdaughter. "I just like to keep everybody else happy. I don't need a birthday dinner and I don't need gifts."

"Nonsense. You should have a birthday dinner, don't you think so?"

"Nee, I don't think so." *Mamm* shook her head.

Levi sat there as quiet as a rock and not saying anything, so Cherish felt it was up to her to come to her mother's rescue. *"Mamm* doesn't like a fuss made."

"Then you and the girls *should* make a fuss of her. She's probably not been made a fuss of and that's why she doesn't like it. You've only got one mother. What do you think, Hope?"

Hope looked up, startled. "Nothing. I didn't say anything."

"You didn't have to. It was the look on your face that said it all."

"Then I'll have to watch the way I'm looking."

"Jah, you will. Does everyone think your *mudder* should have a birthday dinner?"

"It might be fun if we have one," Cherish said, doing her best to either have everyone agree, or end the subject. She could barely stand Ada's droning voice any longer.

"It's not meant to be fun for *you,* Cherish. Not everything is about you."

"I didn't say it was. I'm trying to help, that's all."

"*Denke,* Cherish," Wilma said.

"Well, what do you say, Wilma?" Ada asked.

"It's not a big birthday for me, though. It's not got a five or zero on the end of it."

"How old would you be, *Mamm?*" Favor asked.

Ada glared at Favor. "You don't know how old your own *mudder* is?"

"I have a hard time remembering how old I am."

Everyone at the table laughed.

Ada continued, "I'd think a girl like you would be counting down the days—"

Mamm interrupted, "I'll be forty-six. I'm getting old, so old."

Levi chuckled. "That's young."

"I still wonder where all the years have gone."

"I thought you were older than that, *Mamm.* About fifty or more."

Ada frowned at Cherish. "She looks older because of all the worry you girls cause her. If my *kinner* had given me half the trouble, my hand would still be sore from hitting them on the backside." She held up her right hand.

Bliss announced, "*Dat* says not everything is solved that way."

Both Ada and her husband, Samuel, frowned at Levi. Again, Ada put her hand in the air. "This teaches children right from wrong, and I will not be dissuaded about that."

Cherish stood up and was just about to open her

mouth with some kind of excuse to leave the table when *Mamm* said, "Cherish, you be in charge of the birthday dinner and then it won't be like I'm giving myself a birthday dinner."

Cherish sat back down. "I'd love that. I'll organize everything. *Denke, Mamm,* for giving me so much responsibility. First Levi and then you. It shows that you trust in me, believe in me."

Mamm frowned. "What are you talking about? What did Levi do to give you responsibility?"

Cherish looked at Levi and he gave her a nod as though it was okay to tell. "He said I could be the one to say when to start harvesting the apples this season."

"Oh, that."

"Jah. What did you think it was?" Cherish asked.

Mamm shook her head. "Nothing."

Cherish studied her mother's face. "It must've been something."

"Nee, it was nothing."

"Cherish, do you think you should be talking to your mother like that?"

"What? I just asked her a question."

"It's the way you talk to her." Ada narrowed her eyes at Cherish.

"I'm sorry if you thought I spoke to her the wrong way, but in my mind, I didn't."

"Such arrogance. What do you think, Levi?"

"I'll talk with her later. Over dinner, we can surely find more pleasant things to talk about."

Samuel patted Ada's hand. "That's right. Leave things be."

"I'll try."

"Should I make the plans to have the dinner on your very birthday, *Mamm*? It's a Thursday."

"I think so. *Jah,* that would be nice."

Cherish nodded and then was careful to keep quiet until she was able to leave the table with no one noticing.

CHAPTER TWENTY-SEVEN

The next day, Cherish got out of working in the shop because of the birthday dinner arrangements. She was to spend the day with her mother. It would take all her self-control not to mention the will.

Could she keep quiet?

"I think Ada's upset she's not organizing things."

"*Nee* she's not," *Mamm* said as she poured them each a cup of hot tea. "Just tell her what she is to cook and she'll do that and bring it here on the day."

"Okay. Sounds good. *Mamm,* I know you don't like talking about Florence, but do you sometimes miss her?"

Wilma stared at her. "What sort of question is that?"

"Just a straight-out question."

Mamm put the cup to her lips, took a sip and slowly

lowered it to the saucer. "I took Florence and her older brothers as my own and raised them. Of course I miss her. She's done such a lot for this family."

That was the first time Cherish had heard *Mamm* say that. "I remember her and *Dat* used to be out all day in the orchard. I miss those days."

"Everything comes to an end. Things have a beginning, a middle and an end. Nothing ever stays the same. That's life."

"You're still here, on the orchard."

"*Jah,* I am. Some days I think about how it was when Florence and your older sisters were still here. I wish they lived closer with their babies."

"But Florence is here with hers."

Wilma smiled. "Iris. She looks just the same as Mercy did when she was a *boppli*. It would be nice to see more of Iris, but it's not easy with the way things are."

"You mean now Florence has left us?"

"That and other things."

Cherish stared at her tea. She didn't really want it. "What are the other things she did to us?"

"She left us to open her own orchard."

"She didn't have that intention when she left, but she does love orchards. So, what else would she do with her time?"

"Raise a family. Now she's an *Englisher,* and she could do a great many more things. A whole new world would've opened up to her."

"I know you think that her orchard is in opposition to us, but it's not. It's not like that."

"Cherish, you're too young to know what's what. Florence didn't do right by us."

"Hmm. Did we do right by her? Maybe one of us wronged her in some way?" Cherish held her breath. And then she looked at Wilma. Was she thinking about the world that she cheated Florence out of?

"You're right. I think I didn't realize how hard she was working for us all. I do regret that now. Next time I see her, I will apologize for not seeing what she did."

"She certainly did everything around here. I don't know how. She's only one person."

"She was a special person," *Mamm* said. "Was, until she left us."

Cherish kept quiet. She wasn't going to get into a conversation about whether or not Florence was still special, when Wilma insisted she wasn't, not anymore.

"Why all this talk about Florence and how things used to be?"

"Because I miss those times. We all do."

"I know you do, but we've just got to face the fact that she's gone and she's not coming back."

"Do you ever wonder what *Dat* thought would happen to the orchard after he died?"

"Nee! I don't think he had any thoughts about it."

She noticed her mother swallowed hard before continuing.

"He would think that it would continue on as it

always had. That's what he expected and that's how it should've been. If Florence hadn't been selfish and left us for love... "

"You could hardly say that's selfish. She couldn't help being in love."

"This is why I can't talk to you about grown-up things. You're too young and silly. You can choose who you fall in love with. She bypassed an Amish man to marry Carter."

"The pig farmer?"

"*Jah.* He was very hurt when he heard what Florence had done."

"But it worked out well, didn't it? She's happy with Carter and they have a wonderful baby. Hopefully, they'll have more. I can't have too many nieces and nephews."

Mamm smiled. "And I can't have too many *grosskinner.*"

Levi stuck his head in the door. "Is someone else having a *boppli?*"

"Not that we know of." Wilma laughed.

Levi said, "One thing I've noticed about you, Cherish, is that you always get talkative when there are chores to do."

Cherish was pleased he seemed in a good mood. "I'm helping *Mamm* choose what she wants to eat for her special dinner."

"I'll keep an eye on her, Levi," *Mamm* said. "She is doing a good job right now."

"Hmm. And, when will I get a cup of hot tea?"

Cherish rose to her feet. "I'll get you one right now."

"Sit with us," Wilma said to him.

He grinned at the invitation and pulled out a chair.

Hinting about the will had gone straight over Wilma's head and with Levi sitting with them, that was the end of it for today. She might have another chance later. It was hard to get a quiet moment alone with her mother.

CHAPTER TWENTY-EIGHT

*A*n uneventful week went by and Cherish breathed a sigh when she finally dried the last dish after her mother's birthday dinner was over. Wilma and the family along with the guests had just eaten a wonderful dinner of cabbage and pork rolls, roasted chicken, cold meats, and pork fillets. There'd also been a wide assortment of vegetables and salads. Dessert was a variety of cakes, including Ada's famous German cherry cake, and ice-cream.

The only guests who'd shown up were Ada and Samuel—as usual—and Fairfax and Adam.

Throughout the dinner, all Cherish thought about was how Florence and Carter were ignoring the will. Surely they should've done something about it by now. Perhaps they decided to leave things be. It wasn't what Cherish would've done but, she reminded herself, she had to respect their opinion.

When it was later in the evening and Samuel and Ada had gone home, Wilma and Levi went to bed. Then the young people were free to talk and tell stories and they did that while enjoying the cool night air outside.

As usual, Caroline went around the corner of the house to smoke. Eventually, everyone gathered around her, some standing and others sitting on the ground.

"Does anyone else want a ciggy?" Caroline asked before she lit up another. No one replied. "What about you, Fairfax?"

He glanced at Hope, before he responded, "No thanks."

"Worried that you won't be allowed?"

"I'd have one if I wanted. I just don't want one."

"Please yourself." She put the lighter to the cigarette and then inhaled.

It looked very cool and sophisticated to Cherish. "I'm too young to smoke."

"I started sneaking my mom's when I was eleven. You're never too young. They say it stunts your growth, but I never wanted to be tall."

"I might smoke when I get older."

Favor scowled at Cherish. "You've never wanted to smoke before."

"How's your father, Bliss?" Caroline asked.

"He'll be all right."

"What's wrong with him?" asked Cherish.

"He's hurt his back."

"I didn't notice. He didn't say anything. He was

184

quiet during dinner come to think of it, but everyone was with Ada talking all the time."

Bliss sighed. *"Dat's* not used to being sick. He's hurt his back before, once, and that's the only time he's ever been sick, as far as I know. He never even gets a cold."

"Is that someone in the kitchen?" Caroline whispered.

"I'll go see who it is. It's got to be *Mamm*. I'll ask her if she needs anything for Levi." Hope got to her feet and headed inside.

"I'll come with you," Bliss said.

Once they left, Caroline said, "Go on, Fairfax! Have a quick one before she gets back. She'll never know."

"It smells good. I used to smoke and then I gave it up. I don't know that I want to start that habit again."

"Jah," Cherish said, "He can't waste money because he'll have a family soon."

"Have a free one before your independent world ends, then." Caroline giggled and held one out to him.

"No, thanks, and I wouldn't say it's like that. I'll be happy to be married to Hope, but I didn't know how much I missed smoking until now."

Hope and Bliss returned.

"Hope, let Fairfax be a man. He wants a ciggy."

"He can do what he wants."

Caroline's head tilted to the side. "That's right, the man is in charge in your community."

Cherish knew that Caroline was trying to make

trouble between Fairfax and Hope. Was this the reason she had wanted to stay on with their family?

"You don't mind if I have one, Hope?" Fairfax asked.

"Do what you want."

He stood up and Caroline handed him the packet and he drew one out.

Hope stared at Fairfax, then she turned on her heel and walked away. The cigarette tumbled to the ground as he ran after her.

Caroline grunted as she picked the cigarette off the ground. "Honestly, I can't believe some people. Someone was just complaining about how much these cost and then he just drops it in the dirt."

"She's upset, can't you see that?" Cherish snapped.

"She must get upset easily." Caroline put her cigarette to her lips and inhaled. Then she slowly exhaled the smoke. "I don't see them lasting long."

Bliss pouted, and said to Caroline, "He said he didn't want to smoke and you kept pushing him."

"I can't help that. Maybe they'd each be better off with somebody else."

Cherish wasn't going to listen to Caroline. "Let's go, Bliss."

"Okay."

When they were halfway back to the front door, Caroline teased, "Off to play with the rabbits, are we?"

Favor stood by Caroline's side and she was the only one who giggled.

Cherish opened her mouth to say something back, but then Bliss pulled on her arm. "Leave it. Don't say anything."

When they walked into the house, they saw Fairfax and Hope with their hands clasped talking on the couch. Not wanting to interrupt them, Cherish and Bliss hurried to the kitchen where they found *Mamm*.

"How's Levi?"

"Not too well. I'm just making him a hot water bottle."

"I remember those. We used to have them when we were younger. Florence used to make them for us."

"Didn't I tell you not to mention Florence's name in this house again?"

"Jah, but that was a long time ago. I thought you were over that now."

"I'll never be over the fact that she left us when she did. No notice at all. She as good as ran away."

Cherish looked over at Bliss.

All Bliss said was, "I remember hot water bottles, too. We had them at our other house. This house is warmer."

Wilma screwed the top on the hot water bottle. "I better get this up to him."

"Can we bring you both hot tea or anything, *Mamm?*" asked Bliss.

"We have some up there already."

When *Mamm* walked out, Bliss and Cherish looked

187

at one another. "Well," Cherish began, "it's too early for bed, and we can't go to the living room or outside."

"Not outside with them. We could stay on the porch and not go around the side where she's smoking."

"Okay."

They both hurried past the lovebirds huddled together on the couch deep in conversation, and stepped out onto the porch. As soon as they sat down, an owl hooted.

"There it is again," said Cherish. "I heard it the other night, too. The night when it was raining after dinner."

"I always hear them."

"Oh. I never noticed until recently."

"It's in the barn, I think. We should see if we can see it."

"Right now? In the dark?" Cherish stared at Bliss.

"*Jah*, why not? There's nothing else to do."

Cherish smiled. "Let's do it." Bliss wasn't so bad after all. With Favor now spending every moment with Caroline, Bliss's company was welcome.

With arms linked and keeping as quiet as they could, they headed to the barn. Once the door was open, Cherish reached around in the dark for the small flashlight that was always by the door. When she found it, she closed the door behind them before she switched it on, so the other girls couldn't see where they were.

Cherish pointed the flashlight up to the loft and it

shone on one of their barn cats. His eyes glinted in a spooky way.

"What say you, kitty cat?" Bliss said. The cat looked at them with his large green eyes opened wide. He didn't move a muscle.

"He's saying, 'switch off the light and let me get back to sleep,'" Cherish said with a laugh.

"Yeah, that'd be right."

"I can't see the owl." As soon as she had spoken, the light went out. "The battery's gone." Cherish hit the side of it and it flickered dimly before going dark again. "Botheration."

"I'm scared. Let's go."

Cherish tossed the flashlight on the floor before they both hurried back to the house.

CHAPTER TWENTY-NINE

*E*arly the next morning, Wilma sent Hope and Favor into town to get something for Levi's sore back. Cherish, Caroline and Bliss were told to work in the shop.

Cherish was still at the *haus,* and she and *Mamm* were filling boxes with apple jam from the kitchen.

"What is it, Cherish?" asked *Mamm* as they were emptying the shelves. "You've hardly said a thing all day. Are you upset about something?"

Cherish felt she could barely hold it in any longer and sighed before saying, *"Nee,* it's nothing." She'd given her word, and she'd keep quiet. Cherish walked outside where they'd left the wheelbarrow, set the filled boxes inside it, and went back into the kitchen. She looked through the window and saw Florence walking toward her. She stared at her curiously, and Florence must've seen her because she waved. Since

Cherish's hands were full again, she gave her sister a nod. *"Mamm,* it's Florence."

"Where?" Wilma rushed to the window and looked out. "It is her. And those *Englisch* clothes don't do anything for her."

"It's just a skirt and top."

"But still... Why is she coming here?" Wilma stared at Cherish.

"How should I know? Maybe she's coming to wish you a happy birthday." Cherish swallowed hard. There was a chance that Wilma would soon learn that her youngest daughter had been snooping in her room. She'd be in big trouble, but Cherish would go through being confined to her room for years if that meant things would be made right. She noticed her mother straightened her prayer *kapp.* "You look good, *Mamm."*

"Do I?"

"Jah, you look fine. Pretty as always."

Wilma smiled. "I'll see what she wants."

Cherish stayed in the kitchen where it was safe.

"You look lovely today, Florence," *Mamm* said when Florence stepped onto the porch.

"Thank you. So do you."

"If you're coming to wish me a happy birthday, you're late."

"Yes, I did remember it was your birthday yesterday, but we haven't been speaking to each other on birthdays, so I didn't know whether I should do or say anything, or send a note."

"Come inside."

"No, thank you. Better if I stay here. I do have something to say and after I say it, you may not want me to be inside."

"What is it?"

Cherish could feel Florence's pain. She wasn't a confrontational woman and she knew this must've taken every ounce of Florence's strength to talk to Wilma. She had strained her hearing and heard them when they greeted each other. Then she only heard bits and pieces of what they were saying.

"It has to do with my father, and a certain will."

After a moment's hesitation, her mother finally spoke. "What about your father and a will? He didn't have one."

"That's not true, Wilma. I've seen it."

"What are you saying?"

"I happen to know that you have my father's will in the house. And you've kept it hidden for years. You hid it because he left the orchard to me."

"How could you make up such lies?"

This was the moment of truth. This was where Florence would drag her in and say she was the one who'd found it.

Florence continued, "I know it's true. I've seen it with my own eyes."

"There is no will. He said he'd make one. He never did."

"Wilma, he talked about it with both Earl and Mark."

"Who did?"

"*Dat*. He talked about it and they both told him they didn't want the orchard so he left it to me."

"That's not so."

"I've seen it. It's true."

"How could you see when it never existed? Have you gone mad? Have you seen a will in your dreams?"

Florence sighed. "I just came here to talk to you woman to woman. I didn't come here to be insulted."

"I'm not insulting you, Florence. If you come here saying such silly things, what am I to think? Except that you saw them in your dreams. I wasn't being rude."

"I could take this further. I know the lawyer who drew up the will. They obviously haven't been informed of *Dat's* death. Don't you know as executor you have certain responsibilities to see that the will is carried out?"

"I don't know what you're talking about."

"I think you do and it's clear you're going to go on denying it, so I'm wasting my time trying to be nice."

"What you're saying is nonsense."

"We both know the truth. I'm willing to save you the trouble of going to court and Carter and I will buy the orchard. We'll pay fair market value."

"Do you think you can come here spouting about a

AMISH MAYHEM (AMISH ROMANCE)

will and that will make us sell? Levi has changed his mind about selling. He's not doing it."

Florence shook her head and Cherish knew her sister would have red cheeks from trying to contain her anger. "It's all wrong, Wilma. You know as well as I that the farm should have gone to me. Do you even feel the slightest bit of guilt about what you've done?"

"Me feel guilty? Don't you feel guilty for leaving your family, your home, the orchard, the shop, and all your duties here to rush off and marry an *Englisher* without a second thought or a moment's notice? You were here one day and gone the next. You've been away from all of us. Your younger sisters looked up to you so much. Don't you feel bad about that?"

"It wasn't like that."

"*Jah,* it was."

"The offer is there to buy the orchard."

"I don't want your offer. I don't want you to step foot on my land again. It's not yours, never has been and never will be." After a moment, Wilma said, "You stay on your side of the fence and I'll stay on mine."

Cherish heard the door close and then Wilma walked back into the kitchen. Cherish stood there not knowing what to do. *Mamm* was furious and would be even more so if Cherish talked to Florence.

Wilma, her face drained of color, stared at Cherish. "What did you hear?"

"The whole thing. I couldn't help but hear it."

"It's not true. None of it. Now, get ready for the

customers. I'll give her enough time to get off our land and I'll walk down to the shop with you."

FLORENCE FELT tears stinging behind her eyes and then they cascaded down her cheeks. She never thought she would be unwelcome on this land where she'd helped raise her younger six half-siblings as though they were her own children. She turned and walked away, distraught and feeling she had nowhere to turn.

Carter didn't understand how she felt about this place. No one was in her corner.

She'd always looked past Wilma's shortcomings. Wilma had always been such a weak woman in body and mind, but Florence didn't know Wilma could be this horrible and unforgiving—and such a big liar.

"MAMM, Florence was talking about *Dat's* will."

"Rubbish. I don't want you to mention that to anyone, ever. And don't talk to me about it either."

"Okay." Cherish had hoped for a peaceful resolution. Now she didn't know what would happen if her mother kept denying it.

Both of them packed more boxes to take to the shop.

"You take this box down with the others, and I'll follow you soon with this last one."

"Okay." Cherish shifted from foot to foot. She knew *Mamm* wanted to stay back and destroy the evidence, but what could she do? Cherish lifted the box and headed outside to add it to the wheelbarrow. She saw Levi outside with the horses, and hoped he was feeling better.

She started toward the shop with the load of supplies, but when she was halfway there, she set the wheelbarrow feet down and hurried back to the house. She noticed Levi looking at her so she kept her head down hoping he wouldn't call out to her.

Once she was inside the house and saw *Mamm* was no longer in the kitchen, she ran up the stairs two at a time and burst through her mother's closed bedroom door. She was right. Her mother was on the bed with the box beside her and she was reading something that looked like the will.

Wilma looked up in shock and quickly laid the piece of paper on the bed beside her, tucking it partway under her skirt.

"What's that you've got there, *Mamm?*"

"Nothing." Wilma hastily shoved the paper back in the box, and snapped, "Why aren't you at the shop?"

Cherish was through with nonsense and lies. "Would that be the will? The one that Florence was talking about?"

Mamm's bottom lip wobbled, looking as though she

was going to cry and then Cherish suddenly felt sorry for her and rushed to put her arm around her. *"Mamm, what's wrong?"*

"I tried to do the right thing. I try to keep everybody happy. Try to keep you girls happy, and Levi happy and heaven knows that that's not always easy." She picked up the end of her apron and wiped her eyes. "I'll tell you something. This is the will, and I know you'll keep it a secret."

"Why would I do that? This is what *Dat* wanted for our family."

"Because Florence left the community."

"But *Dat* died years before that."

"A girl her age shouldn't have been responsible for the running of the orchard."

"She did a fine job of it. *Dat* showed her what to do. She did it for years by herself."

"We all helped."

"By herself, in charge of it, I meant."

"Don't you see, Cherish? What would've happened to us? Your *vadder* wasn't a practical man with many things. He made a good job of the orchard, but he made mistakes sometimes. Because of his mistakes we had to slice off our property and sell the cottage—the one where Carter and Florence are living now. He wasn't a perfect man."

Cherish considered her mother's words. She'd always remembered him and thought of him as perfect, but of course no one was.

"I've done the right thing. I'm sure of it. I wanted us all to have a home here forever."

"Nee, Mamm. We would've had a home here for the rest of our lives." As soon as it slipped out of her mouth, Cherish knew she'd made a big mistake.

Wilma's eyes grew wide and she stared at her. She pushed Cherish's arms away from her and stood up. "You knew what the will said!"

Cherish's jaw dropped open as she searched for words. None came.

Wilma pointed to her. "It was you who told her about the will."

There was no use denying it. Cherish nodded. *"Jah,* it's true."

"How could you do that to us … to me?"

"Well, it all started because Levi kept saying the place was his. He's making all the decisions, but isn't it your orchard too? He talks as though it's his and not both of yours and that's the very least he should do. Say it's both of yours, I mean."

"What does it matter what he says? It's all of ours. What have you done, you silly girl? You've ruined everything."

Cherish hung her head. She didn't like to upset her mother, but the truth had to come out.

Wilma huffed. "I did what was best. I had to. I didn't think it was right a girl her age to be left everything. Just as I don't think it's right for Aunt Dagmar to leave you her farm."

"But those were *Dat's* wishes, and they were Dagmar's wishes. Can't you see that?"

"I can see it, but I don't agree with them. I can't do anything about you inheriting the farm since you refuse to share with your sisters. I'm still cross with the bishop in that community for taking you to the lawyer to have everything finalized without my knowledge."

"It wasn't like that. He was probably trying to save you some work and probably save you the trip."

"But still, you were a minor at the time."

"I still am, but we're not talking about me, we're talking about this place belonging, well, it should belong to Florence. You've taken away her inheritance. Aren't you worried *Gott* will punish you?"

"*Nee*, I am not! I did what was right so what could be wrong about that?"

Cherish stood up and took a deep breath. "I think you're distracting yourself and justifying yourself by talking in riddles."

"Justifying myself?"

"That's right. *Mamm*, there is nothing right about what you've done. It's illegal for starters, and it's morally wrong."

"What you're worried about is man's laws, but we don't live under the law of man, we live under the law of *Gott.*"

Cherish sighed. Surely her mother knew this was wrong. "Somewhere in *Gott's* word it says we should abide by the rules of the land, doesn't it?" She needed

Joy there to know where that part was. She'd know the exact chapter and verse.

Wilma shook her finger at her. "This is what's going to happen. You're going to keep quiet, for all our sakes."

Levi appeared in the doorway. "Keep quiet about what, Wilma?"

CHAPTER THIRTY

*B*oth Cherish and Wilma stared at Levi.

"You're up the stairs. Is your back better?" Wilma asked, forming her lips into a smile.

He stepped further into the room. *"Nee,* my back's the same, but when I saw Florence walking past the house in tears and neither of you mentioned anything about Florence even being here, I suspect something's going on. And when Cherish goes halfway to the shop, leaves the wheelbarrow of products, and rushes back to the *haus,* I *know* something's going on. What is it?"

Cherish didn't know what to do. She wasn't going to be the one to tell him. All she did was put her hand up to her mouth.

"See what trouble you've caused, Cherish?" Wilma snapped.

Levi frowned at Cherish. "I might've known. What have you done now?"

"I've done nothing. I found something, that's all."

Wilma pushed the box a little further away from her. "You had no right to be in this room or go through my things."

"You're right. I'll go to my room and think about what I've done."

"It's all right, Cherish, you can go," Levi said with a nod.

Wilma grabbed her hand and pulled Cherish down to sit on the bed with her. "You can stay. You've caused all this trouble. I think you have some explaining to do."

"Can't you tell him, *Mamm?*"

"This is your fault. When things go bad around here and I mean really bad, it'll all be your fault. You'll only have yourself to blame."

Levi rubbed his back. "Will someone tell me what's going on? I don't care which one of you tells me."

"*Mamm* might put it in a better way." Before either of them said anything, Cherish stood and then bolted past Levi and ran to her room. Instead of closing the door, she left it open a little. She had to find out what Levi thought of all this. At least now she knew that he had nothing to do with it.

Then she heard Levi's voice. "Are you going to tell me or do I have to guess at what's going on?"

"It's his will."

"Whose will?" Then there was silence. "Oh. *His* will."

"Jah."

Cherish found it strange that her father's name was never mentioned by either of them. He was always referred to as he, or him, or Wilma's first husband. It was odd.

"And, what about it?" Levi asked.

"I put it out of my mind completely."

"Oh, Wilma." There was silence for another moment. "Let me guess. Cherish found her father's will."

"That's right. I should've destroyed it, burnt it years ago."

"Wilma, this is our orchard, our livelihood. You've got to fix this. Who was the orchard left to? I'm guessing by the look on your face it wasn't you." When Wilma didn't speak, Levi said, "Was the orchard left to his sons, Mark and Earl?"

"Nee. Not exactly."

"Then who?"

"It was left to just Florence."

"Just Florence?"

Cherish felt sorry for Levi. This would have shocked him greatly and it did going by his high-pitched voice just now when he found out the orchard should've belonged to Florence—a woman he seemed to despise for no reason.

After another pause, he asked, "Can I see it?" There were sounds of rustling paper, and then silence before

Levi spoke again. "You'd go against your husband's final wishes?"

Cherish was relieved. He didn't agree with what she'd done either.

In her whiny voice, *Mamm* said, "I forgot it."

"You can't just forget something like this. Be honest with me."

"I was just trying to do what was best for the family. We were left on our own with no man to look after us." Her sobs echoed through the hallway to Cherish's ears.

"This can't be ignored, Wilma. I don't know where this puts us now. When I married you, I took care of you and this family the best I could. I thought the income from the orchard would help me support you all. There aren't many men who would take on a woman with as many children as you have. The money has to come from somewhere."

"You have money. I know you do."

"I have a couple of houses, as you know, and the rest of the money is loaned out to people in need."

"What are you saying? Are you saying that if I'd had nothing, no orchard, you wouldn't have married me?"

"That's something we will never know now, isn't it?"

Through sobs, *Mamm* said, "I thought you loved me."

"Right now, Wilma, the only thing I feel for you is amazement. You look like the woman I married, but the Godly woman I married would not have done this."

"Don't be angry with me. What are you going to do?"

"Was Florence here because she wants the orchard?" Levi asked.

There was silence, Wilma must've nodded her answer.

"She could go to a lawyer. This is awful news and we've got that reporter looking for stories about us. He'll find out what's happened when we move off the orchard."

"Nee, we can't leave here. We can just carry on as though nothing has happened because nothing has changed, not really."

"Everything's changed, Wilma. Can't you see that? The orchard was never really ours, never yours. He left it all to Florence."

"It's all Cherish's fault."

"Nee, Wilma, it's your fault. No one else's. This never should've been hidden."

"It's in my name now, so let's just leave things be. Florence will see sense in time. If she was serious about claiming it as her own, then surely Carter would've come with her today."

"Right now," Levi said, "all I have to say is, the last thing I want is to go to court."

"Me too. That would be the absolute last thing I want."

"Wilma, you made this mess, you should be the one to get us out of it."

"What does that mean? What do you want me to do? I can't do anything on my own. What will I do?"

"My back's hurting. I need to try to get down the stairs again. I did my best to be a good husband and a good provider. I looked the other way when your *kinner* annoyed me and were disrespectful, but a man can only take so much."

"What..."

Cherish listened intently, but heard no more words. The only sounds were the closing of a door and heavy footsteps going down the stairs. A few seconds later, she heard the faint sounds of her mother's sobs.

CHAPTER THIRTY-ONE

*C*herish sat on her bed wondering if she should've done nothing when she saw that will. All it had done was upset people. Florence and Carter seemed at odds with one another and now Levi was so upset with *Mamm*.

A gentle knock sounded on Cherish's bedroom door. She sprang off the bed and opened it to see her mother's tear-stained face. "Oh, *Mamm*." Cherish put her arms around her and Wilma cried on her daughter's shoulder.

"I have to do something."

"What?" Cherish asked.

"I have to put this right for all our sakes."

"But how?"

Wilma shook her head. "I'm not sure. We'll wait until your sisters come back from town, and then will you walk with me to Florence's house?"

"Sure."

"I don't want you to come in with me. Just walk me there and back again. Best you don't hear what's said. I must confess what I've done. Then I'll see what they say."

"Okay. If that's what you want."

"It is. In the meantime, get the wheelbarrow down to the girls at the shop and make sure they're doing okay. Then come back here."

Cherish did as her mother requested.

The girls returned from town an hour later. Cherish heard their loud voices. When Cherish walked out of the kitchen there were no girls in sight and Levi was leaning against the wall with his eyes half-closed. She rushed to him. "Are you okay?"

"Just tired."

"Where are the girls?"

He could only speak in a whisper. "I don't know."

"Sit down."

He moved his head, indicating no.

"Mamm!"

Mamm came running down the stairs. "Are you ready to go?"

"Jah. First help me walk Levi to the couch."

Wilma frowned when she looked at her husband. "What's wrong?"

"Nothing. Just tired."

Wilma called for Caroline and Favor, and they came running.

"You're supposed to be looking after Levi."

"Sorry, *Mamm*," Favor said. "We were coming in a minute. Hope and Bliss are working in the shop now. Caroline and I don't like being split up. We've got the muscle cream for him from the pharmacy."

"Good. As soon as I put some cream on his back, Cherish and I are going out for half an hour. Don't leave Levi's side in case he wants something. And be quiet so he can rest."

"Okay."

Wilma shooed the girls into the kitchen so she could massage the muscle cream onto her husband's back. With an arm around Wilma, Levi walked to the couch, sat while she applied the cream, and then lay down with a deep sigh. Wilma called Cherish back from the kitchen.

"How's your back, Levi?" Cherish asked.

"Still there."

Cherish was surprised he was trying to be funny when he seemed so ill. "Is it still hurting you?"

"*Jah*, it is."

"Do you want me to stay?" Wilma asked.

"*Nee*. You go."

"He'll be fine, *Mamm*. We'll watch him."

"Yes, Mrs. Bruner, we'll be here."

Wilma nodded and then patted Levi on his shoulder.

Cherish found Caramel sitting on the porch and closed him in the house so he wouldn't follow.

Then Wilma and Cherish set off to the next-door property to talk with Florence.

"I do hope they're home," said *Mamm* as they made their way through the orchard.

"I'm worried about Levi. Do you think he'll be okay?"

"*Jah.* He's strong, never gets ill. He's just pulled a muscle."

"Bliss said he never gets sick."

"He's not sick."

"He looks a funny color. Kind of gray."

"He's fine."

"I hope everything goes okay. I mean, what will they say? What are you going to say? Florence wants the orchard and, as you know, it should've been hers."

"Just stop talking for once! I'm trying to think," Wilma snapped. "You never stop talking."

"Just filling in the silence. That's all I'm doing."

They walked through the orchard with neither of them speaking. Cherish held the barbed wire fence wide for Wilma to get through. Then Wilma held the wires for her.

Once they were on Carter and Florence's land, they both stood and looked at the cottage.

"This cottage used to be ours once and the land on it. It was a wasteland back then, but they've fixed the drainage and breathed life into it. Good for them."

"I know. *Dat* had to sell it when we had some bad years in the orchard."

"We had some tough times when you and your sisters were younger, but we got by."

"I know."

Her mother turned to her, with her jaw clenched. "Stop saying that you know! You don't know. You think you know everything, have every answer, but you don't. You're still a child. The sooner you go to your farm, the better."

She knew her mother was only nervous about having to face what she'd done and it was best she didn't respond.

"You wait here. What I have to say most likely won't take long."

"Okay. I'll stay right here." Cherish sat on a clump of grass.

Her mother gave her a disapproving stare. "Don't get grass stains on your dress. You know how hard they are to get out."

"I won't. It'll be fine."

"Pray for me, Cherish."

"I will. I'll do that."

Her mother left her sitting there and then walked up to the house. Cherish knew what it felt like to confess one's sins. It wasn't pleasant. She felt bad for her mother. Confessing something awful she'd done had always been worse than taking a dose of castor oil.

Cherish gathered some pebbles she found on the ground, five of them, and threw them in the air and tried to catch them all on the back of her hand. All but one landed on her hand. She tried it again. When she was bored with that, she remembered she was supposed to be praying for her mother. She closed her eyes and said a prayer, asking *Gott* for everything with her mother to go well, for a good outcome, and for everyone to get along.

CARTER LOOKED out the window as he sat drinking coffee with Florence in the kitchen. "Hey, we have visitors. It's Wilma plus one bonnet sister."

"Are you sure it's Wilma?"

"It's her all right. And Cherish, but she's sitting down on the ground just this side of the fence line. Wilma's nearly at the house."

Florence joined him at the window. She'd just finished telling Carter what had happened with Wilma and he'd been able to calm her down. "She's probably coming to deny it again."

"You don't know that. She wouldn't be coming here to upset you again."

"I hope not."

"Let's just hear her out. It's best if this can be solved amicably."

Florence blew out a deep breath. "I know."

They both walked to the front door and opened it. A few seconds later, Wilma was in front of them. Wilma swallowed hard and said nothing, just stared.

Carter said, "Are you here to talk about the orchard and the will?"

"Yes, I am."

"You'd better come in and sit down," Florence said. "Iris is asleep upstairs so this works out well. We can both concentrate on what you have to say."

Once they were seated, Wilma put both hands in her lap and took a deep breath. "I was wrong."

That was the last thing Florence expected to hear. If Wilma was admitting she'd done wrong, then surely she was going to pass the orchard over. Both she and Carter kept quiet, waiting for Wilma to continue.

"I was wrong to hide the will. I was scared. I was the mother and left as the only parent to nine children. I think—I thought—he should've left it to me. I was also hurt that he didn't discuss it with me." Wilma wiped away a tear that fell down her cheek. "I'm not trying to excuse myself. There is no excuse, but I am now admitting I'm wrong." She looked into Florence's face. "Levi has asked me to fix this. I know he won't be happy living there now that he knows the truth."

"You can all still stay there, still get a living from it. I'm not trying to change things for anyone. I just want it to be run properly, and..."

"I understand," said Wilma.

Florence could feel from the way Carter was looking at her that something didn't sit right with him. This was her orchard, though, and her father had understood that. Why didn't Carter, the man she loved, know her heart? She didn't want the financial gain. All she wanted was what was hers.

Suddenly they all heard screaming coming from outside. Carter jumped up and raced to the door. A breathless Cherish and Favor were running toward them.

"It's Levi," they both screamed.

Florence and Wilma rushed out the door and Wilma elbowed Florence and Carter out of her way. "What's wrong?"

Favor yelled out. "He's not breathing."

"Has anyone called 911?" Carter asked.

"I think so."

With Wilma frozen in shock, Carter ran inside and grabbed his cell phone. As he ran back to the Baker house with the girls, he called for the paramedics.

Wilma hurried after them and Florence set off running too. Then she stopped abruptly.

Iris. I have to get Iris.

Florence turned around, ran back to the house and up the stairs, and bundled her sleeping baby. Then, hugging Iris to herself and praying, she walked quickly to her old home to see what was wrong with Levi.

When Florence got through the thick layer of trees, she saw Levi lying on the ground outside the house and a small crowd had gathered around him. Wilma was wailing and Cherish was doing her best to console her.

A woman was kneeling beside Levi. She leaned over him and Florence saw she was performing CPR.

Florence guessed the woman had been one of the customers of the shop. How else could anyone get there that fast? What a blessing she had medical knowledge.

By the time Florence reached the crowd, the woman was sitting back on her heels. "He's breathing on his own now. His pulse is erratic, but fairly strong. The paramedics won't be far. I'll stay until they're ready to take over."

Thank you for reading Amish Mayhem. I hope you are enjoying the series.
To stay up to date with my new releases and special offers, add your email at my website in the newsletter section.
https://samanthapriceauthor.com/

Blessings,
Samantha Price

THE AMISH BONNET SISTERS

ABOUT SAMANTHA PRICE

USA Today Bestselling author, Samantha Price, wrote stories from a young age, but it wasn't until later in life that she took up writing full time. Formally an artist, she exchanged her paintbrush for the computer and, many best-selling book series later, has never looked back.

Samantha is happiest on her computer lost in the world of her characters. She is best known for the Ettie Smith Amish Mysteries series and the Expectant Amish Widows series.

www.SamanthaPriceAuthor.com

Samantha loves to hear from her readers. Connect with her at:

samantha@samanthapriceauthor.com
Facebook - SamanthaPriceAuthor
Follow Samantha Price on BookBub
Twitter @ AmishRomance
Instagram - SamanthaPriceAuthor

Made in the USA
Las Vegas, NV
10 April 2021